SECONDHAND BRIDE

THE ALMOST WIVES CLUB, BOOK 2

NANCY WARREN

AMBLESIDE PUBLISHING

ISBN: ebook 978-1-928145-12-7

ISBN: print 978-1-928145-13-4

Cover Design by Kim Killion

Ambleside Publishing

CHAPTER 1

*A*shley Carnarvon was dragging a single black sock out from under Eric Van Hoffendam's bed when he proposed. Which meant, given her position, hips in the air, feet wedged against the wall to give her leverage to reach the pesky sock, that he proposed to her butt.

In fact, most of what he'd said sounded like a radio announcer's voice coming from another room. He slapped her lightly on the part of her that was in his line of vision, and she backed out, sock firmly in hand, to ask, "What did you say?"

Eric lounged against his headboard, his blond head just-woke-up sloppy. He was a great-looking guy. On his best days, he looked like Ryan Gosling. Not Ryan all dressed in a tux to go to the Oscars, more schleppy Ryan, the guy who looked like he'd either just got out of bed or was thinking of going to bed. Eric was bearded; mostly, she thought, because he was too lazy to shave.

In fact, Eric was pretty lazy about most things. In a family of wealthy overachievers who made the Kennedys look like a bunch of dilettantes, he was definitely bringing down the average. He liked to party, he liked to sleep in, he liked to spend his days pretending to look for a job while generally hanging out.

Ashley was the official Carnarvon family slacker, so they suited each other perfectly. Even though he was twenty-six years old, he still lived in his old bedroom in his parents' mansion. He snuck her in some nights as he'd been doing on and off for nearly ten years, since she was sixteen.

He wore a gray T-shirt over pajama bottoms and, while she'd been dressing, he'd opened a stack of mail. He held out a wedding invitation. She squinted, but it was hard to decipher the words through the scrolls and curlicues of the font on the wedding invitation. It was as though even the printer was excited about the wedding. "Melissa and Douglas?" she guessed. They were mutual friends who'd announced their engagement last fall.

He shook his head. "Donovan and Kylie."

"Wow, wedding invitations already? They just got engaged!"

He tossed the invitation aside and rolled toward her. He had a twinkle in his eyes that he usually got when he was about to pull a prank. For a lazy man, he put a lot of energy into his pranks. "I said that it feels like everybody we know is getting married. Maybe we should, too."

She pulled her sock on, yawning. She'd love to lounge in bed all day but she had to get to work. It was only barista work, but it helped pay her expenses. Unlike Eric, she didn't have a cozy trust fund to fall back on. "We should do what?" She'd kill for a cup of coffee but the unspoken rule was that her nighttime visits to Eric didn't exist. So she always left discreetly, retrieving her bike from behind the bushes against the back wall of the grounds and letting herself out onto the private drive so she could bike home.

"Get married!"

She dropped the boot she was holding so it clunked to the floor. She turned to stare at him. "Get married?"

"Yeah." He didn't look like he was joking. He looked slightly pink in the cheeks like he might actually be blushing.

"You and me? To each other?"

"Why not? We like each other. We've been hanging out together since high school. You're a cool girl."

"Your parents would never let you marry me. They're the worst snobs on the planet."

"Why wouldn't they like you? You're a Carnarvon."

"Only because my loser dad never got around to marrying my mom. I have no money, no trust fund, no decent job. I live in a shack on my uncle and aunt's estate. I'm a charity case."

He reached out and traced her arm with a fingertip. "Come on. It'll be fun. We'll throw a huge party. My parents always said they'd buy me a house when I got married."

"You want to get married so you'll get a house?" This was not the Eric she knew.

"No. I don't know... I want to get on with my life. You and me, we're both stuck. I think we could help each other out. We've been together ten years. I think we should get married."

It wasn't like they'd been boyfriend and girlfriend for a decade. She'd always thought of it more as a friends with benefits relationship that they pursued whenever both of them happened to be single. His parents had always looked down their noses at her and she'd never once been invited to a family event. She was convenient to him, as he was to her.

Still, there was something appealing about the idea of both of them getting out from under the heavy weight of family disapproval.

He gave her the white-toothed grin that always undid her. When Eric turned on the charm she'd do pretty much anything he asked. "I love you," he said.

"You love me?" This was the first time he'd ever said those words.

He shrugged, clearly uncomfortable, and pulled at the edge of a pillow. "Sure. Obviously. Don't you love me?"

"I—" She'd been part of Eric's life forever. She knew all his bad points as well as his good ones. He was a youngest child, a charmer who gazed around cheerfully, cracking jokes, pulling pranks, waiting for good things to rain down on him. And mostly they did. When he smiled at her she felt as though good things were raining down on her, too. She'd always loved him, of course she had. So, she nodded. "You know I do."

He jumped off the bed and threw his arms up in a victory dance, he jumped and gyrated his way around the bed, then he picked her up and swung her around, kissing her, a big smacker on the lips. She was giggling helplessly when he put her down.

"Come on," he said. "Let's go celebrate."

"Celebrate? It's eight in the morning."

"I'll buy you breakfast, then we'll tell my parents. I can't wait. They'll be so happy."

She wasn't so sure about that. "I can't go for breakfast. I have to work."

He made a *pffft* sound. "Blow it off. You just got engaged, you can take the day off."

"Not if I want to keep my job." Which she didn't, actually, but she needed the cash. "Besides, you should tell your parents on your own. In case they hate the idea."

"They'll love it," he said with complete confidence. "Trust me. Come for dinner tonight."

She kissed him swiftly. "Call me later."

"How do you feel about Tahiti for the honeymoon?"

"Why not?" Then, she and her newly engaged butt got on her bike and wheeled home in a daze.

The big gates of the Carnarvon estate were open for a delivery truck, so she pedaled past and rode down the path to the old gardener's cottage where she'd lived all of her life, or as much of it as she could remember, with her mom.

The smell of brewing coffee met her as she entered. Score.

"Hi, hon," her mother called from her bedroom. Soft music played and she knew her mother was writing her morning pages. Melody Carnarvon had taken a writing course years earlier that promoted morning pages as a way to unleash creativity. Her mother had stuck religiously to her morning pages, which were basically a journal. If her creativity had been unleashed, Ashley had seen no evidence of it.

She poured coffee into the green pottery mugs they both favored because they were huge, and took the coffee in to her mom's room.

At forty-seven, Melody Carnarvon was in a constant struggle against time and gravity. Ashley thought her mom looked great, with a yoga trained body, hair that was still long and blond, and pretty blue eyes, but her mom spent a lot of her time and most of her money on attempting to stay young.

"Morning," she said, as Ashley passed her a mug of coffee. "Oh, thank you. I really should drink more green tea."

She said this most mornings but still drank her coffee.

Ashley settled on the end of her bed and sipped her own coffee, hoping a jolt of caffeine would get her world to make sense again. "I need to talk to you."

"What's up?" Her mom put down her journal. The current notebook was bright blue and featured dragonflies.

"I think Eric Van Hoffendam just proposed to me."

Her mother was as surprised as Ashley had imagined she'd be. "What? Eric proposed? Like *marriage* proposed?"

"I think so."

"Well, what did he say?"

"He talked about how a lot of our friends are getting married, which is true. He flapped a wedding invitation at me. Then he said, we should do it. Get married."

Her mother was listening so intently she wished she had a

more romantic tale to tell. But Eric wasn't much for romantic gestures. "And what did you say?"

"I think I said, 'yes.'" But when she recalled the conversation she couldn't be sure.

"You're not pregnant, are you?" Melody didn't say it in a judgmental way. The same thing had happened to her, without the benefit of a marriage proposal.

"No. Of course not." She hoped she was smarter than her mom had been.

Her mom sat there for a second, and then jumped up and down on the bed from her sitting position, careful not to spill her coffee. "Oh, my God. You're going to marry Eric Van Hoffendam?"

She felt like this must all be happening to someone else. "Yes... Yes. Unless it was some kind of practical joke."

"Nobody jokes about getting married."

If anyone did it would be Eric, but she'd known him forever and she was certain that he'd been sincere. "I guess not."

"I can't believe it!" Melody slapped her free hand to her cheek. "There's so much to do. To plan." She set down her coffee and grabbed up her journal, turning to a blank page. "A list. We need to make a list. Let's see, a date of course. Have you set a wedding date?"

She laughed. "Mom, I've been engaged about thirty-five minutes. I haven't decided anything."

"Well, we need to start thinking about these things. Good venues book up ages in advance. It's not every day my only daughter gets married." Then her eyes filled with tears. "Oh, honey, I'm so happy for you."

"And you think it's the right thing?"

"Of course, I do. Eric's a great guy." Then her tears turned to laughter. "And please let me be the one to tell Duncan. I want to watch my brother's face when I tell him that his niece is getting married, after his precious son pretty much got jilted at the altar and made a complete fool of himself."

She'd never forget that performance. After Ted and Kate Winton-Jones had broken up, Ted suddenly grew a pair and announced to his parents that he was in love with another woman. He'd insisted on bringing her to dinner, and Millicent had invited Ashley and her mother to join them, probably hoping that if she invited more people over then Duncan would have to be polite.

She'd never forget that meal as long as she lived.

Ted had walked in with a woman who was older than him by at least a decade and looked as though she did all her shopping in the East end of Melrose Avenue.

Long red hair in ringlets, heavy makeup, the gravelly voice of a smoker.

Marlene was her name. Seeing Ted try and make his parents like this woman, well, it was the only time she remembered feeling sorry for her big cousin.

The evening had ended in a yelling match the likes of which she hadn't seen before or since. Ted had stormed out and sworn he'd never come back.

Later, he'd texted her and asked her to pack up his stuff from the pool house where he'd been living. Since she didn't have a driver's license, she'd had to ask Eric to help her take the boxes of Ted's belongings to their secret meeting spot, a Starbucks parking lot.

Within days, the cleaning staff had gone in and scoured out the pool house. Now it was as though Ted had never stayed there.

He still worked at the family firm and she imagined one day the drama would end, but for now she knew her mother would enjoy telling the oh, so perfect Duncan and Millicent that Ashley was marrying into a family even more prestigious than theirs.

She hadn't done very much right in their eyes. It was funny to think that marrying a slacker like Eric was a real coup in the Carnarvon world.

If she was really going to marry him. Eric wasn't like Ted. If his parents didn't approve of his choice, and she couldn't imagine she was their dream bride for their son, then the wedding was probably off.

She headed to the coffee shop where iced mochachinos, soy lattes, half-sweet, skinny, no whip hot chocolates kept her too busy to think of much other than the end of her shift.

On her break, she pulled out the sketchpad she always had with her and flipped to a blank page. She began designing wedding rings for her and Eric. They weren't traditional, naturally. She knew a jewelry designer and had some ideas on matching rings that would be inexpensive but really, really cool.

Assuming Eric's proposal hadn't been a practical joke.

CHAPTER 2

*W*hen Ashley got home that afternoon, her mother was on the phone. Their house phone, which hardly ever rang. She widened her eyes when Ashley walked in. "Absolutely, Grace. Ashley and I are looking forward to it. Yes, six is fine."

She hung up and they looked at each other. "That was Grace Van Hoffendam."

"And?"

"She invited both of us to dinner tonight."

"How did she sound?"

"Like she was delighted to welcome you into the family."

"Really? What did she say?"

"That she was delighted to welcome you into the family."

"Huh. Guess I must be delightful, then."

Her mom hugged her with one arm. "You are a piece of perfection. My work is done. Oh, good thing I've made my list. I spent all afternoon on websites, and I got a few books on wedding planning." She gestured to the couch where a stack of books leaned precariously next to a fan of bridal magazines. "I want the Van Hoffendams to know that we'll plan a great wedding."

"But mom, we can't afford—"

"Hey, you're my only daughter. You're getting married. We'll figure it out." Her mother was looking seriously happy. "Oh, and the best part of you getting engaged on a Saturday morning is that Duncan wasn't at work. I made an excuse to pop by the big house."

"Really? Borrowing a cup of sugar?"

"Please. You give me no credit for subtlety. I asked if they had any bridal magazines or wedding planning books I could borrow."

"Queen of subtlety, that's you."

"I know. So, naturally, they wanted to know why I wanted such a thing, and, naturally, I told them that their niece is marrying into the Van Hoffendam family."

"How'd they take it?"

"After Duncan recovered the power of speech, he said mostly nice things."

"Mostly?"

"He might have mentioned the lack of job factor on Eric's part, but he soon saw the positive. You know, an alliance with another powerful family."

"And Aunt Millicent?"

"Not sure she ever recovered the power of speech."

It was so nice, for once, to be the model of perfection and for her cousin Ted to be the one screwing up. "I'm sorry I missed it."

"Me too. But, they want to throw you and Eric an engagement party."

"Wow. That's so nice of them."

"I know. Get used to it. You marrying Eric puts us back in the club."

"Is it a club we want to belong to?"

Her mother shrugged. "The food's always good."

The strange sense that her life had suddenly been turned inside out continued that evening when they arrived at the Van Hoffendam mansion for dinner and she and her mother were greeted at the front door by the Van Hoffendams' maid.

For all the times she'd snuck in the back way to Eric's room, she could count on the fingers of one hand the times she'd come in by the front door. And usually, Eric had been with her.

But, when they were led into the living room where Eric and his parents were waiting for them, she'd have thought, from the welcome, that she was already part of the family.

Grace Van Hoffendam said, "Oh, my dear, let me have a hug." And pulled Ashley into her scented embrace. Eric's father, a bearded, scary looking man who resembled Sigmund Freud, only taller, shook her hand and muttered, "Pleasure."

They treated her mother like an old friend and soon the five of them were sitting over glasses of expensive champagne. "To Eric and Ashley," Charles Van Hoffendam said solemnly, and they all sipped.

She'd ended up seated beside her mother, with Eric and his folks across from her. But when she caught Eric's eye he winked at her.

"We're very excited about the news," Grace said. She'd clearly had a recent Botox session, for there was no discernible change in expression on her face.

"And I couldn't be more thrilled," her mom replied. "Eric and Ash go way back."

"Good." Grace leaned over and picked up an elegant notebook off a priceless antique table beside the priceless antique couch. She uncapped a pen that would no doubt one day be a priceless antique itself. "I've taken the liberty of engaging a simply wonderful wedding planner. She did the Halliburtons' daughter's wedding last year, you know, and they were thrilled with her. Here's her card."

She passed the elegant little card, which looked like a mini wedding invitation, to Melody.

"Wow. Thanks."

"And here, I wonder if you could proof this ad. I've booked space in all the papers to announce the engagement." This time, Grace passed over a prepared advertisement. Ashley peeped over her mother's shoulder and read that the Carnarvon family and the Van Hoffendam family were delighted to announce the engagement of Ashley Elizabeth Carnarvon to Eric Charles Van Hoffendam. And then there was a paragraph about each of their illustrious families. Very little about Eric or Ashley, and nothing at all to indicate that Melody was a single mom.

"Naturally, as soon as we can get these two to sit for their formal engagement portrait, we'll put that in the papers too."

Formal engagement portrait? She glanced at Eric and he shrugged and made a face, but so subtly no one but she could see it.

"Wow. That's incredible. I was planning on doing a lot of the organizing myself," her mother said, sounding slightly intimidated.

"I only offer her services. We'll cover her expenses of course." She glanced at her husband.

He picked up the hint, cleared his throat and leaned forward. "Melody, we perfectly understand that your circumstances are more modest than our own, so we'd be very honored if you'd allow us to pay for the wedding."

"Oh, no. I couldn't do that. Thank you, but Ashley's my daughter. I've dreamed of her wedding for most of her life. I've got this handled."

"At least let us contribute. Since we'll be inviting a number of friends and business acquaintances, it's only fair."

"Oh, well... We can talk about details later."

She shot another glance at Eric. They'd never talked about the actual ceremony. Well, they hadn't talked about the wedding at all and now the entire thing was being organized without anyone even asking them what they wanted.

He was either attempting to count the bubbles in his champagne flute, or he was avoiding eye contact.

"My brother and sister-in-law want to throw an engagement party for Ashley and Eric," Melody said, obviously happy to have something to contribute.

"Wonderful. We'll look forward to it."

Then another maid announced dinner and they were ushered into the formal dining room. The food was delicious, and Grace and Charles were excellent hosts, but she never stopped feeling that she had to be on her best behavior.

Grace and Melody did most of the talking, in full wedding planning mode. "I don't think a long engagement is necessary when these two have known each other so long, do you?" Millicent asked, looking at Melody.

"How soon were you thinking?"

"It's April now, let's say an early June wedding."

Ashley swallowed too fast and nearly choked on an asparagus tip. All of her friends who got married took at least six months, usually a year. What was the rush?

Melody also looked confused. "But if we want to book a good venue, it takes at least six months."

"Oh, were you thinking of booking somewhere *public?*" Grace asked, as though Melody were suggesting they get married in a public bathroom. "I was thinking a garden wedding at home. Of course, if the Carnarvons don't want to host the wedding, we'd be happy to have it here."

She and her mom exchanged glances, but she had no idea what to say, and Eric didn't seem like he was even listening.

"I think a garden wedding would be beautiful."

After dinner, Eric said, "Would you like to take a walk outside with me?"

"Yes, sure." She glanced at her mom and got a nod of approval.

She and Eric walked out through huge French doors to the ornamental gardens closest to the house. The Van Hoffendams' gardeners kept their topiary trees perfect. They were shaped like animals prowling beneath giant ornate pillars. One memorable night in high school when his folks were away, Eric had got hold of a sculpting saw and remodeled the pillars so they looked like huge erections. Their friends had loved it and his shares on Facebook had been in the thousands. His parents were not as amused.

And here was the man who carved trees into pornographic shapes staring down at her in all seriousness. "I wanted to give you this." He pulled out a ring box from his suit jacket pocket. Her heart began to thud. This was all too real.

"It was my mother's," he said, his voice deep and reverent as though she'd died giving birth to him instead of being perfectly healthy and currently sipping brandy in the living room fifty feet away.

He flipped open the blue box and there was a ring she remembered well. "My father gave her this when they got engaged."

"I know. I remember it. She wore it all the time before the ring got upgraded to a bigger model on their thirty-fifth wedding anniversary."

He dropped the serious and went for teasing, "Stick with me for thirty-five years and you'll get upgraded too."

He took her left hand and slipped on the ring. It was a perfectly nice diamond solitaire, exactly suitable for a newly engaged couple, and frugal since Eric didn't have to outlay any money. Just completely not what she would have chosen.

Still, she wasn't going to complain about the diamond ring a man had put on her finger—not with all their parents standing by—so she thanked him, let him drag her behind the decorative hedge and maul her for a couple of minutes. He took her hand to lead her back inside but she held him back. "Why is your mother in such a rush to get us married?"

He held her left hand out so the light caught it, making the unfamiliar ring sparkle. "I think she's just excited. We can wait longer if you want. Up to you. But after ten years, it's not like we don't know each other."

"I guess." Something felt slightly off, though. "Everyone's going to think I'm pregnant."

He grinned down at her. "If I drop enough hints, I bet I can get you a baby shower."

"Don't. Even. Think about it," she warned him, then laughed when he pulled her in for a noisy kiss.

AFTER EVERYONE HAD OOHED and *aahed* over the ring, including the hired help, brought in like extras to pad out a scene, she and her mom left.

As they drove home, her mom glanced over at her. "Phew, that was intense. I think the entire wedding got planned in one evening. But that was so sweet the way he surprised you with the ring."

She fingered the diamond on her left hand. "I know. I wish I'd been warned, though, so I could have squeezed in a manicure today. And what's with the big rush?"

"When you and Eric were outside, Grace confided in me that she thinks you'll be a steadying influence on Eric. They've told him now that he's got responsibilities, he's got to get serious about a job."

She stared at her mother. "She must be thinking of someone else. No one has ever called me a steadying influence."

"Don't sell yourself short."

When they got home, Ashley discovered her day of surprises wasn't over yet.

She opened the door, which they never bothered to lock, seeing as they were on a secure compound, and said, *"Oh."*

A wedding gown on a dressmaker's form stood ghostlike in front of them. The breeze from the door opening caused the skirt to ruffle slightly as though the dress were alive.

"What is it?" her mom asked when she stopped dead. When Ashley didn't say anything, she pushed past her and echoed her daughter. "Oh."

Melody recovered first and walked in. "There's a note attached." She picked up the note and read aloud: "Consider this our engagement gift, Ashley. A wedding gown designed by Evangeline. She's looking forward to your first fitting. Much love, Millicent and Duncan."

"Wow," her mom said with more enthusiasm than a cheerleader on speed. "They gave you a wedding dress!"

Ashley fingered the gorgeous silk. "Not a gift, a hand-me-down."

CHAPTER 3

"*Y*ou always have to make things hard," Lester Sprague yelled.

Bennett Saegar sat down. When his agent started yelling at him, he knew he wouldn't get a word in edgewise until the torrent subsided. Besides, a media van was blocking the entrance to his own house. It didn't look like he'd be going anywhere for a while.

"I don't want to make things harder," he protested, but Lester wasn't listening.

"I told you not to cast that nutcase, didn't I? But do you listen to a guy who's been in the movie business since before you were a glint in your father's eye?"

"I didn't cast her. I write the scripts. I'm not a casting director."

"You wrote the damn script with her in mind and told the producer you did it!"

Okay, he couldn't argue with that. Vanessa Moore had a waiflike, lost quality, an ethereal beauty that had inspired the character of Vivien in his screenplay for *The Last Girlfriend*. Ben hadn't realized that what he'd seen projected on screen was the real deal. Vanessa wasn't acting. She really was waiflike, lost, and (okay, Les had a point) a nutcase. "She played the part brilliantly," he put in, just to remind Lester that, artistically, his instincts were good. But Lester barreled right over that argument.

"Of course she was. She's nuts. And now she's killed herself over you and the press is going crazy. What the *hell?*"

"She's not dead, Lester." Thank God.

But Lester wasn't interested in seeing the positive side of this mess. "Be better if she *was* dead. If she gives one more interview telling the world how she loved you and you scorned her, your career won't be worth shit."

In fact, more offers were coming in than ever before, and who knew that better than his agent? Seemed being a screenwriter who made actresses suicidal was good for the career, even if it was hell on his personal life.

"Can't even get near your own house. Place is swarming with media and lookyloos. More crazies looking to stalk you, I bet."

The fact that Vanessa had chosen to end it all in his bed had made him and his home the focus the type of media hype he loathed. He was almost certain she'd imagined that her act of despair would result in him realizing he couldn't live without her or some such crap. Unfortunately for her, she hadn't checked to make sure he was home before breaking into his house, putting herself, naked, in his bed, and downing an entire bottle of sleeping pills. By the time he'd come home an hour later, it was almost too late. In all the madness of getting her to the hospital he hadn't noticed the pathetic suicide note until the next day.

Didn't matter. He could read it in a dozen places online. Her first act upon returning from near death had been to circulate copies of her suicide note to the media. Maybe her spelling and grammar weren't much, but Vanessa was an imaginative creative writer.

She was now "recovering" in a private facility, which, unfortunately for him and any intellectually sound person, allowed patients internet access as well as visitors. Even if those visitors were reporters or bloggers.

Vanessa was milking her near death for all it was worth, painting him as a villain. While she didn't ever come right out and say he'd seduced and abandoned her, she insinuated as much. And she was so pathetic and waiflike and all the rest of it that he couldn't speak publicly without coming across as the very bully she'd painted him as.

"I don't want you talking to anybody, you understand? Not the media, not the bloggers, not friends in the industry. Nobody."

"Don't worry. I'm hiding out for a while." And that pissed him off as much as anything. He'd been accused of something he'd never do, and now the paparazzi were making his own home enemy territory.

"Good. Where?"

"I'm staying in a family friend's pool house."

"It better not be a woman friend. I'm telling you now, you might get away with this if that miserable shiksa survives, but only if you live like a monk for the next year."

"A year? That's a long time to do penance for writing a part that was perfect for an unbalanced actress."

Lester snorted. "Let this be a lesson to you. You find me a balanced actress and I'll show you a divorce lawyer who isn't a schmuck. They don't exist."

"Yeah. Got it."

"Where is this pool house?"

"Malibu."

"Good. You're still close to LA if I need you." He heard a wheezing cough and knew Lester had been smoking again even though his doctor, his wife, his ex wife, all three of his kids and his assistant had all been bugging him to quit. "What are you doing at this beach house?"

"Working on a new script." That would make Lester happy. "And there are no women in it. Only men, and most of them get killed."

"Good. You finally working on that noir thriller?"

"Seemed like a good time."

A wheezy chuckle answered him. "Okay. Keep your balls in your pants and we might get through this."

Now that the rant was over, Ben settled back. "Thanks, Lester."

"I got your back."

HE HAD to sneak out of his own house, the house he'd had designed and built after his first success. Now he was creeping out like a burglar carrying a suitcase containing a few clothes and another crammed what was basically his office in a bag. He had a great office in his house. Now he was going to be working in somebody else's pool house. Not that he wasn't grateful. If he checked into a hotel he could too easily be found, but hidden away in Duncan Carnarvon's pool house he was as good as invisible. And so he would stay until some other media whore grabbed the spotlight away from Vanessa.

Ben had been hiding from the paparazzi, and people who seemed to have nothing better to do than hang around watching his house, for days.

He left in the wee hours of the morning, when everyone had gone home to rest up for another day of Ben-baiting. He took his beloved convertible with him and sped down the relatively quiet streets of LA and out to Malibu. By the time the sun rose, Ben was unpacked and walking along the beach in peace. He could think on the Carnarvon's estate, he could walk without feeling eyes on him and whispers behind his back. And, he hoped to hell, he could write.

The story had been burning within him for a while. It was more violent than his usual fare. The main female character was a fickle, faithless wife who died a violent death, and right now that absolutely suited his mood.

He had some ideas for act one, some snippets of dialogue, and, as he walked, he felt the calm breath of the ocean echoed in his own breath. He walked for a long while, letting ideas play in his head. He'd had enough of real life drama. He wanted to get back to the movies where stories made sense.

He headed back to the pool house, ready to put on a pot of coffee and get his working day started. The best thing about his hideout was that no one knew where he was except Lester, and his parents who had arranged the temporary home for him. He was far from the craziness, far from all writing distractions, and best of all he was far from women.

He strode up the path ready to get to work.

And he stopped dead.

There was a mermaid in his pool.

He blinked and the mythical creature resolved itself into a woman in a green bikini. The light had caught her so she sparkled, but she was a woman, strong legs powering her forward. An athletic one too, based on the clean, efficient strokes that carried her quickly through the water. She reached the end and flipped with as much grace as any mermaid he could imagine. Now she was heading his way, the pool rippling blue and green around her. She got to the end, and—did she see his shadow? Sense his presence? She put her hands on the edge of the pool and raised her head to look up at him.

Droplets of water rolled down her face and the years rolled away with them. He hadn't seen Ashley Carnarvon in a decade but he still remembered being the object of an intense crush.

Ashley had followed him around like the lonely, lovesick teenager she was for all of one summer. No one had developed an obsession to rival it until… Vanessa.

His first thought was, *hell, no*. Not this. Not now. Of all the pools in Malibu, she had to swim into his.

For a second neither spoke. He was aware that she'd filled out since her teenage years. A diamond nose ring sparkled. She projected a certain go-to-hell attitude that she'd been trying on when she was fifteen. Her vulnerability had been achingly obvious back then. Now she either hid it better or had toughened up. He hoped it was the latter. And God, he hoped she was over her crush. Otherwise he'd be searching out somebody else's vacant pool house within the hour.

"Ashley?" he asked, adding a note of uncertainty even though he knew exactly who she was.

"Ben?" She returned the question, even though he knew she was as certain about his identity.

He nodded.

Her forehead creased in puzzlement. "What are you doing here? Ted's not here anymore."

"I know. I'm staying in the pool house for a while."

"You're staying *here*?" There was a big uplift on the last word, as though she was more than surprised. Maybe as horrified to find him here as he was horrified to find her.

"Yeah. You okay with that?" Might as well find out now if there was going to be an issue before he typed 'Act One, Scene One, *Fade In*.'

She tossed her head and a spray of water scattered. "Yeah. Why wouldn't I be?" she responded, all tough girl and I-eat-boys-like-you-for-breakfast.

"No reason."

"Okay." There was a tiny pause. He had no idea how to fill it. Finally, she said, "You mind if I swim in your pool? I come out here most mornings."

"No. Of course not. And it's not my pool, it's your uncle's. He said I could stay here for a couple of weeks. I'll be working." Which he hoped she took as a hint not to be dropping by for coffee.

"Good luck," she said as though she couldn't care less. And then, with a wave and a splash, she was powering through the pool in the opposite direction.

He stared after her. How had he never considered the possibility that Ashley Carnarvon would still be living with her mother at her uncle's place? He knew his math was right when he calculated her age at twenty-five. Ten years since he'd been a twenty-year-old college senior, full of himself, and she'd been the teenage girl who worshipped him. Did she really still live here? With luck she only dropped by to use the pool.

With luck. And luck sure hadn't been his close companion lately. Who could he ask to find out if Ashley had ever shown suicidal tendencies?

He could still hear her rhythmic splashing as he strode up the path to the entrance of the pool house and walked inside. It wasn't large, but it had everything he needed. Namely, a power source, Internet connection, a rudimentary kitchen and a full sized bathroom. There was a king sized bed in a separate room. Big windows overlooked the pool, and the bar was bigger than the kitchen.

He set up his computer on the kitchen/dining table, a bamboo and glass affair that seemed to be all the rage in beach-house décor. He poured himself a mug of fresh coffee and settled into the oversized bamboo armchair that made him feel as though he were at a resort in the Bahamas.

He powered up his computer and opened a new file:

Act One, Scene One. Fade In.

The main view from the pool house was, naturally, the pool. There were louvers above the big picture window that he'd left open, as he found them. They let in fresh air. They also let in the sounds of a swimmer.

Fade In.

Sounds of a gun fight.

How could he think about a gunfight on dark, gritty streets when the sounds of a California girl swimming laps in a pool were drowning out his concentration?

He contemplated shutting the louvers but that would mean he had to stand in front of the window and she'd probably hear or see what he was doing. He didn't want Ashley Carnarvon thinking she had any effect on him whatsoever. He'd get used to the distraction. It was a pool house. People were going to be swimming.

He grabbed the leather journal where he kept notes and reminded himself to invest in some earphones. He never worked to music like some writers did, but he'd get the kind that doubled as earplugs. He made a note of that, then went back to his laptop.

Fade in.

Sounds of a gunfight.

Wide shot of a warehouse. Interior shot. Meat packing plant.

Seriously? Meat packing plant? Where had he studied film? The college of cliché?

He deleted the phrase.

The sounds of splashing slowed to a few drips. He glanced up without intending to, to see Ashley haul herself out of the pool in one graceful motion that highlighted strong, lean arms, a muscular torso, and a backside that made his mouth go dry. She got to her feet and grabbed a big, blue beach towel. He could see the water running down her body. A gorgeous body. Athletic and toned. Nothing waiflike about her. Her ample breasts were showcased by the green bikini. A belly ring sparkled.

She was a solid woman, with hips and thighs and curves

where curves should be. As he stared like a fool in a peep show, her gaze rose and before he could thrust his attention back down to his computer screen, she was staring into his eyes. He saw challenge, and an attitude that said louder than words, 'what do you think you're looking at?' If she were a kid she'd taunt, "Why don't you take a picture? It'll last longer." But they weren't kids. And he was pretty sure he had snapped a mental picture that would last much longer than he wanted it to.

ASHLEY TOOK her time sauntering back to the cottage she shared with her mom, on the outside acting as though she hadn't a care in the world, but inside she burned with humiliation. Maybe a decade had passed but she hadn't forgotten the way she'd followed Ben around the summer he'd come to stay. She'd been crazy, out of her mind crazy about the guy. At twenty, he had seemed wildly sophisticated, and she could still remember how he'd looked bare-chested, laughing as he and Ted headed out surfing. He hadn't kicked her to the curb when she'd been so obviously smitten with him. He'd been nice to her in an I-feel-sorry-for-the-lovesick-loser way that was somehow worse than if he'd been cruel. At least then she'd have recovered from her crush a lot faster.

Well, she was grown up now and, luckily, engaged to be married, so he could take his pervy gaze and shove it. It had been nice, though. There'd been that one moment when she caught his gaze on her, and even through the plate glass window she'd known he was seeing her as a woman. Finally. He was still hot. Hotter now he was all grown up. But she was getting married soon and that hot Hollywood screenwriter could write her out of his script.

CHAPTER 4

*B*eing the poor relation sucked, Ashley thought as she was pinned and tucked into her hand-me-down wedding dress. On the plus side, the fancy gown had cost many thousands of dollars and was a designer one-off. On the minus side, it looked like crap on her.

"And to think, it's never even been worn," her mother gushed, grateful as always for the handouts of her illustrious relatives.

"Not sure that's a big bonus in a wedding dress," she said. Who could forget the drama and intrigue when the Most-Perfect-Bride-Ever, Kate Winton-Jones had scampered off right before she was to be married in this very dress dumping Ted Carnarvon on his smug ass? Ashley chuckled at the memory. The normally placid Carnarvon family had been more fun than a reality show for a while.

"I can't believe you're actually getting married," her mother continued, pretending she hadn't heard the snarky comment. Ashley and her mom used creative deafness a lot to keep their relationship smooth. Her mother had a kind of wistful look in her eyes. She'd never had a wedding of her own; the prince who was Ashley's father hadn't waited around long enough and for some reason Melody never got too serious about another man after that.

"Neither can I." She felt a little fluttery looking at herself in the triple mirror, but that could have been lack of oxygen. She must be at least a dress size larger than Kate.

She gazed at her reflection and felt as though she were finally finding direction in her life. She'd marry Eric, finish her degree, get some kind of job, maybe have kids.

It was surprisingly fun being engaged. People said nice things and asked her where she was registered, which meant gifts. She'd never even had a home of her own and now she and Eric were choosing everything from cutlery to china to linens. She'd talked about going away to college, but it was so expensive and her mom didn't have the money. She didn't feel like taking on a lot of debt, so she stayed at home and went to local college and worked part time.

It was going okay, but the idea of having a husband and a home with new things in it was kind of intoxicating.

At that moment Evangeline breezed into the fitting room of her Rodeo Drive salon. Even though Ashley had seen her in countless magazine ads and on TV, Evangeline was still breathtaking up close, as though she'd rushed off a photo shoot to check on the gown.

SHE SWEPT FORWARD. "I don't think I've ever had a second bride in one of my gowns," she said in her clipped British accent, not sounding very pleased with the idea.

She scanned Ashley from her deep blue eyes until it was all she could do not to squirm.

"My inspiration was a lily," she said sadly.

All of them gazed again at her reflection. She did not

resemble a lily. Her breasts were too large, her hips too round. This lily was bursting out of its vase.

"Nothing to be done," she said finally, turning to Melody. "Luckily, we've got Darling Delores to take the photos. That woman can make an elephant look slim. Really. It's a miracle."

An elephant?

"We're really happy you could get her for the wedding," Melody said. Then, like the loyal mother she was, she said, "And I think Ash looks beautiful in the dress."

"Well, obviously. But not, I think you'll agree, like a lily." The designer picked up Ashley's hair and held it over her head. "When you go to the salon, tell Guillaume that I want the hair piled on the head. Up, up, up. Tell him he may need to add a hairpiece. We want the illusion of height." She pulled Ashley's hair straight up and stared critically at her reflection. "Yes. Good."

After a few brusque instructions to the two seamstresses working on the gown, Evangeline turned and swept back out again.

"God," she said to her mother, "What a terrifying woman. I'm not wearing a hair piece."

A quiver went through one of the seamstresses busy marking the places where the seams would be let out. It could have been laughter or terror, no way to tell.

"*Shhh*," her mom said, glancing back. "We'll talk about it later."

"I'm going out later. And luckily there will be alcohol."

Her mom grinned at her. "Wish I was going drinking. Grace and the wedding planner are coming to the house and, with Millicent's help, we'll figure out where to put the tents and the gazebo for the wedding."

"Do you need me?"

"Do you want to be involved?"

"No... I'm doing other important wedding stuff. First, meeting with the bridesmaids."

"Getting them drunk before you tell them about their duties? Or after?"

She made a seesaw gesture with her hand. "We'll see how it goes."

Sienna and Whitney were her two best friends and they'd always said they'd stand up at each other's weddings. None of them would have guessed she'd be the first to marry. She arranged to meet them at Wainright's, one of their favorite hangouts downtown. The beer was cheap, the décor was funky and the crowd was young.

She got there first and secured a table. Sienna showed up a few minutes later. Her hair was wet, and things trailed out of her backpack where she hadn't stuffed everything in properly. "Sorry, am I late?"

"Not very."

"Drinks are on me tonight," Sienna said, motioning to the waitress. Whitney joined them at that moment. "Champagne," she announced. "We're celebrating. I can't believe you're getting married."

"I know."

When the champagne was poured, Sienna said, "To Ashley for getting married and to Whitney and me for being awesome bridesmaids."

"To us," Ashley said and then sipped her drink.

Whitney leaned forward. "So, let's see the ring."

She showed them and they dutifully admired the solitaire.

The three of them settled in and took a few minutes to catch up, though they all posted to social media enough that there wasn't much they didn't already know about each other.

Whitney was an articling student who also taught yoga and lived with Bradley, the neediest male Ashley had ever met who was weaned.

Sienna was interning at a music magazine and spent most of her time at parties, which she claimed was an important part of her business. She called it networking. Ashley called it drinking on the company's dime. Not that she was complaining. Sienna had invited her along to a few of the events and they'd been a blast.

"I am so glad to have some time with you two. I feel like my life has been taken over by other people organizing this wedding," Ashley said.

"I know. And we're totally here to help." Whitney looked as though she'd have blown this evening off if she could have. She probably had briefs to prepare from the down dog position while cradling Bradley and telling him everything was going to be fine. Bradley was a struggling musician, or at least he called himself that, though the most struggling he seemed to do was getting out of bed in the morning.

"You're my best friends, so I can tell you anything, right?" she said, leaning in.

"I knew it!" Whitney cried to Sienna. "Didn't I say?"

She leaned forward and dragged Ashley's glass to the center of the table. "And you shouldn't be drinking in your condition. Don't you ever read those signs posted in public bathrooms?"

"I am not pregnant!" she yelled.

A guy was walking past holding a beer mug in each hand. "Do you want to be?" he asked, looking ready to volunteer for the job.

"No!"

"Kay. If you change your mind, I'll be over there."

Seriously flustered, she dragged her drink back and took a hit.

"What is it you want to talk about?" Sienna asked, as though Ashley being pregnant had never crossed her mind.

"Making sure you save the date and figuring out when we can look at bridesmaid dresses."

Whitney pulled out her smartphone. "Good, I'll schedule the wedding in now. When is it?"

"Seven weeks from Saturday."

Whitney stopped and stared at her. "You're definitely not pregnant?"

"No! Our mothers are all excited and seem to be planning the entire thing without us."

"That happens all the time," Sienna said. "People always say it's the bride's day, but from what I hear, it's the mother's day."

Whitney nodded. "Okay, scheduled. And I found this great new bridesmaid app for listing out and planning what we're each supposed to do."

"Great," Sienna said, pulling out her own phone. "Send me the link and I'll download it too."

"Dresses." Whitney sighed. "You don't have much time. You need to get your wedding gown first."

"I have my wedding dress. Evangeline designed it."

"Oh, I loved her in that movie," Sienna said, "that British one. She's gorgeous. I hear her wedding dresses are impossible to get and cost more than a facelift."

"All true, but I already have an Evangeline gown."

"Holy crap. Really? An actual, designed-by-Evangeline creation?"

"Yes." She drank more champagne. She and Whitney and Sienna went way back, but like most of her friends who'd grown up in their zip code, they were rich. Even though they totally got that she wasn't, it was still hard sometimes to admit how much of her life had been handed down. "Remember when my cousin Ted was supposed to get married? And didn't?"

"Hells yeah," Sienna said. "It was the big gossip at the golf club for weeks."

"Golf club?" Whitney asked.

"My mom and dad are addicted."

"Anyway," Ashley continued, "Evangeline designed a

wedding gown for Kate Winton-Jones, the girl Ted was marrying."

"Didn't she run off with a guy she picked up in a bar?" Sienna asked.

"I heard *he* ran off with a hooker," Whitney answered.

"Anyway, the point is, that the dress ended up at Duncan and Millicent's place. Kate didn't want it and her mother didn't want it, so Millicent gave it to me for my wedding."

"Wow, pretty nice gift."

"I know. I had a fitting today." She pulled out her own smart phone. "I got my mom to take some pictures of me in it."

They eagerly grabbed her phone and put their heads together over it. Whitney scrolled through the four photos her mom had snapped. "What a gorgeous dress," Sienna said at last.

"It looks like crap on me, doesn't it?"

Sienna was a terrible liar. Her face kind of squished up and she didn't look at Ashley when she said, "No, it's weird to see you all dressed up like that is all. Not your usual style." She shook her head. "I can't believe you got an Evangeline gown." She glanced up. "This is really happening, isn't it? You and Eric?"

"Sure seems like it is."

Whitney pulled out a tablet computer from her big bag. "Let's be efficient about this. I bet we can find bridesmaid dresses online and order them in our sizes. Such a better use of our time than spending a day shopping."

While she scrolled, Ashley said, "Can you make it to the engagement party? That's two weeks from now."

Whitney's forehead creased. "I can move some things around and at least make an appearance."

Sienna nodded. "I'll be there for sure."

"Good."

Then they leaned in. "Okay," Whitney said, "so tell us everything. Where are you going to live? Honeymoon?"

Sienna raised her eyes from the tablet's screen. "You didn't even tell us what he said when he proposed. I want all the details."

Luckily, since her proposal story was the least romantic in history, Sienna was easy to distract. "That guy at three o'clock is totally checking you out."

Sienna tossed her hair then didn't seem sure which way to look. "Really? My three o'clock or your three o'clock?"

"Mine."

While Sienna pretty much searched the full clock face, Whitney, the more practical of the two, said, "Now that Ted's not living in the pool house, can we crash there on the night of the engagement party?"

She felt warmth crawl up the back of her neck but tried to play it cool. "No. Didn't I tell you? A family friend is staying in the pool house for a few weeks."

"What friend of the Carnarvons' would stay in a pool house?" Whitney asked. The Carnarvons' friends tended to rent yachts or other mansions if they needed temporary shelter.

They were going to find out anyway, since he'd be at the party, so she said as casually as she could, "Bennett Saegar. The screenwriter."

Sienna forgot about three o'clock guy and stared. "Bennett Saegar that you were in love with and never shut up about all summer back when we were, what, seventeen?"

"Fifteen. I was a kid. I had a little crush."

"Oh, my God. Is he still gorgeous?" She turned to Whitney. "Remember how hot he was? Isn't he a screenwriter now?"

"He was totally hot." She pulled out her tablet once more and did a Google search for him. She laughed out loud. "Check this out. He's in a hottest young male writers list."

She passed the tablet to Ashley who nodded. "Yep, that's him."

"How could you not tell us that the love of your life is living in the pool house?"

Yeah, why hadn't she? Probably because it was so insignificant. She shrugged. "He's there to write. I barely see him." Except every single morning when she went for her swim. He was usually at work already, and he'd wave. She'd wave back. No biggie.

CHAPTER 5

*A*shley headed home after the girls night out. Bradley had come by the club to drive Whitney home and they'd given her a lift. She let herself in through the man door in the big gates and trod softly down the path that led by the pool house. A few decorative lights lit her path, which she knew so well she could navigate her way home in complete darkness.

If the pool house wasn't occupied she'd be tempted to strip down and jump into the cool water. She'd skinny dipped a million times in this pool after hours. Uncle Duncan would freak if he knew. But no one knew. It was her little secret. However, now that Ben was in the pool house the skinny-dipping wasn't going to happen. She'd take a quick shower before bed.

But, as she walked by the pool house, she heard low, sinister words that had the hair standing up on the back of her neck. "Why don't you tell me everything you know, and die easy?"

Probably Ben had the TV on. Still, she crept around to peek into the window. Holy Crap. There was a man standing in the main area. And he was holding a Beretta 38 caliber pistol. He was pointing it at someone who was out of her range of sight from where she stood in the shadow of the bushes.

Shit. She'd learned how to shoot when Ted had expressed an interest and she'd been invited along to the gun range. She'd turned out to be a good shot and to everyone's surprise, shooting had become a hobby. She knew enough about guns to be very nervous about what was going on in the pool house.

She fumbled in her bag, *call 9-1-1* pounding through her brain, but her phone was dead. Why was her phone always dead when she needed it?

"Go ahead and kill me. Won't get you what you want." Oh, no. That was Ben's voice. Didn't he know the first thing about survival? He lived in LA! Don't piss off the guy with the gun.

Gun. Right. She sprinted to the cottage, grabbed her Walther PPK. Bullets. She fumbled in bullets so fast that more fell on the floor than made it into the magazine.

She raced back to the pool house, heart pounding, half terrified she'd hear the thud of a shot. She slowed to peek into the front window. Good. No one was dead or bleeding. The dude with the gun said something in a low voice. Taunting.

She had no idea whether the pool house door was locked, but she knew where the spare key was kept. She eased the key out from under the flower urn, its hiding place for as long as she could remember. Her hands were shaking but she managed to unlock the pool house door. Then she reminded herself of every gun lesson she'd ever attended. Breathe deep. Hold still. Then fire. She breathed deep. Nerves were her enemy. Of course, it was one thing to be calm on the practice range. Quite another when someone's life was in danger.

"I swear to God, if you don't tell me where you stashed it, I'll kill you."

She had her back to the wall as she eased herself close to the main room. She couldn't see Ben but she could see the guy with the gun.

She aimed first, from the doorway, before he saw her, and then ordered, "Drop the gun."

The guy turned to her, shock in his face, his eyes opening wide and his jaw going slack. But he didn't drop the gun.

"Do it!" she yelled, clicking off the safety and advancing into the room.

She had never shot anything more alive than a clay pigeon, but in that moment, when someone she cared about was in danger for their life, she knew she could do it.

The guy must have read her deadly earnest for he dropped the gun. It made a thud when it hit the ground. Even though she hadn't asked him to, he held up his hands in surrender. "What the f—"

Ben stepped forward. "It's okay, officer," he said to her in a calm tone. "You can stand down."

But she hadn't been born yesterday. She did a visual search of the room. Still holding the gun trained on the guy with his hands in the air, she backed toward the closed bedroom door, opened it fast and glanced inside. Only when she was certain that there was no one else in the pool house did she click the safety back on and lower her weapon.

Ben had never taken his eyes off her. Neither had the perp. "Is that gun loaded?" he asked.

"What could I do with an empty gun? Throw it at him?" Her tone was scornful, mostly because adrenalin was kicking in.

"You know how to shoot that thing?"

Oh, how she wished they were at the shooting range so she could show him. She gave him a withering stare instead. Because Ben wasn't rushing to dial 9-1-1, or thanking her for saving his life, she had to accept that she'd gate crashed something that she had no business being part of.

"Who's the bitch?" the guy asked, dropping his hands now she'd lowered her gun.

"Ashley Carnarvon, meet Mike Konister. Mike's an actor. We were working on a scene."

"Working on a scene?" Her voice rose, mostly because she was angry and embarrassed in equal measure. "You use a Beretta to play a scene? Couldn't you fake it with a banana or something?" Now that her legs were starting to shake, she needed to sit down, and the fact that the two of them had put her in this awkward situation pissed her off even more. "I could have killed you."

Ben spoke again. "He's very method."

"Method almost ended up dead on the floor."

Ben seemed genuinely interested. He said, "Couldn't you shoot him in the leg or the shoulder or something?"

Gun guy said, "Do you mind? I'm standing here and this bitch still has the gun."

She shook her head. "Way harder than you think. He moves, I move, the gun shoots a little to the left, there is no way to be that accurate. The rule is, if you aim to hit someone you aim center body."

"I gotta go." Mike Konister said. He started to reach down and then glanced at her warily. "You going to blow my head off if I pick this up?"

She didn't like him and she thought he was an ass to wave a gun around while shouting threats even if he was running lines.

"Let me see it," she said, walking over and picking up the Beretta before he could. She removed the clip. It was empty. Good. She handed back the two pieces. "Playing with guns can get you killed," she informed him, sounding like a schoolteacher.

"I'm outta here," he said.

"Thanks Mike, I'll call you."

"You want to run lines again? We do it at my place." And then he left, banging the door behind him.

There was complete silence for a moment. Now she saw the

scattered manuscript pages, with lines crossed out and scribbled over. Being a Good Samaritan was one thing, crashing a script reading with a loaded weapon was in another category. "I should go, too."

"Wait," Ben said. "I'm pretty sure I locked the door. How did you get in?"

She contemplated telling him he was mistaken but somehow she knew he wouldn't believe her. She pulled the key from her pocket where she'd shoved it when she let herself in and handed it over.

He looked at the key in his palm. "Where is this kept?"

"Under the planter pot. Third from the left. Always has been."

He nodded, squinting his eyes half shut. She guessed he hadn't known about the hidden key. He bounced it on his palm a few times. "You know I'm a screenwriter, right?"

"Your job description kind of slipped my mind when I saw a guy waving a gun and threatening you." She thought back to her responses, realizing how much of her reaction had been instinctive, but honesty compelled her to say, "My mind did flash to that scene in *Home Alone* where the kid plays bits of an old gangster movie to scare the bumbling thieves, but when I peeked through the window I saw a real gun."

"So you broke in here believing my life was in danger?" He didn't sound grateful or impressed, just sort of surprised.

She didn't feel like explaining herself or defending her behavior. Now that the fight-or-flight reaction was passing she knew humiliation would soon follow. "Looks like it."

He regarded her for a moment. "So, I guess you've still got a monster crush on me, huh?"

She was so surprised at his words that she felt her jaw go slack. Then she saw the wicked glint in his eyes and realized he was teasing. Maybe she still had a ton of adrenalin to get rid of, but this seemed like the funniest line in the world. She felt a snort of laughter rise up and didn't bother trying to suppress it. It felt good to laugh. To her surprise, he joined in. And she realized he'd said exactly the right thing to break the strange tension that had gripped the pair of them since he'd first turned up here.

When her last giggle subsided, she said, "I did have a horrible crush on you. Thanks for reminding me of how I humiliated myself right after I tried to save your life."

"You were a nice kid. But I was too old for you."

Since she really didn't want to delve into the details of a period in her life she preferred to forget, she changed the subject to something that would interest him.

"So, you're writing some kind of murder mystery?"

"More a dark vision of justice, and where does the line between right and wrong blur. Good cops, bad cops, drug wars, turf wars. You like that kind of movie?"

"I like movies that have women in them."

He blinked at her. "There are women in my movie."

"Correction, I like movies where women aren't either victims or bimbos."

"Why do you think I'd write women that way?" He sounded aggravated.

"Because it's what men do when they write movies like the one you're describing."

He turned back to his computer and started banging keys. "Here, come. Grab a seat." He pulled out a wicker chair and snugged it up beside his, then centered his computer between the two seats.

"What are you doing?" She stayed where she was.

"I'm finding a scene with my main female character." He was scrolling and she felt him change as soon as his focus was on the words on his screen, as though he became Bennett Saegar the screenwriter and not Ben, the guy who was hanging out at her uncle's pool house. "You can read it and tell me if you think the female character sounds real to you."

"Really?" she felt honored that he'd want to share this with her. A little nervous that she'd blurted out something she was going to regret.

The chairs were stupid big; she felt like she was on a bamboo throne when she wedged herself into the seat. The one good thing was that the wide chair arms put her and Ben at a distance. Still, that only meant that she had to lean in, and he had to lean in, so they could both see the screen.

Her mind flashed back to the results of Whitney's Internet search earlier and how Ben was one of the hottest young male writers in the country. She had no idea who invented lists like that but she had to agree. Especially when he had this intense vibe going, his eyes keen with intelligence and his hair tangled where she suspected he'd been running his hands through it.

He pushed the laptop over to her and said, "Read this scene. Tell me what you think."

"I don't know anything about your movie."

"She's the wife of the police chief and she's sleeping with the head of the drug gang he's trying to crack."

"Nice girl." But she read the scene. Then she went back and read it again. Even though she was extremely conscious of Ben's intent gaze she refused to rush or let herself get rattled. He'd asked for her help and she wanted to give it. Besides, if she had a chance to influence even one male-oriented Hollywood movie in favor of women, she wasn't going to blow her chance.

"Well?" he asked when it was pretty clear she'd finished reading through the scene a second time. She liked that he was anxious for her opinion, as though her thoughts mattered.

"How old is this woman?"

"Late thirties."

"And why is she sleeping with the drug guy?"

He leaned in, all intent and sexy. He wore a blue shirt with the sleeves rolled up, revealing powerful forearms that he hadn't developed from typing. "It started out as revenge sex because her husband had an affair and she wanted to hit him, and hit him hard. But now she's developed feelings for the drug lord."

She nodded. "She dies, right?"

He jerked in his chair. "Probably. Yeah."

"Of course she dies. Women like her always die in movies. First, she's a bimbo for sleeping with a dangerous man who could not only wreck her marriage, but kill her or her husband or probably both. Then, she becomes a victim." She pushed his laptop back without bothering to say, 'Told you so.' She felt it was implied in the heavy silence between them.

"Okay, smartass. How would you do it?" he sounded kind of pissed.

"I'd never write a movie like this, how do I know?" Then she relented. "But I can tell you she would never say that line." She leaned over him and pointed at the line on the screen, then read it aloud: "You make me feel young again."

"Why not? He does make her feel young." He sounded genuinely interested in her opinion.

He might be one of the hottest young male writers in the country, but he did not know women. "My mom is forty-seven, a decade older than your heroine, but she's a good example. Your unfaithful wife is just entering that stage in her life when age is starting to catch up with her." She put her hands out. "You've met my mom. Can you imagine her saying to a guy she was sleeping with that he made her feel young again? She might feel it, in fact she probably would, but she'd chew her own head off before she'd put the age thing out there. Women like my mom, and, I think, like the woman here, hate getting older. They hate losing their looks. So they spend a lot of money on facial treatments and join gyms and work on a fantasy that they aren't getting any older."

She put her head to one side, thinking. "She might talk about aging with the women in her beauty treatment place, but she'd never say it to a guy she wanted."

"So, what would she say?"

She felt a grin pulling at her mouth. "I don't know. You should ask my mom."

"Funny." But he didn't look very amused.

"I'm sorry, did I wreck your scene?"

"No. You probably saved it, but I hate that I was so blind." He sat back. And in that chair it was a long way back. "I think I've been really stupid."

"Hey, it's one line of dialogue. You're overreacting."

He shook his head. "Not about that line. I think you're right. I put women in categories. God, I never realized I do that. Could have saved myself a hell of a lot of hassle if I'd noticed that before *Ravensong*."

He shifted as though a dozen bamboo rods were poking into his back, which was possible, but she suspected something else was making him uncomfortable. "Does this have something to do with why you're here?"

"You seriously don't know why I'm here?"

She snorted. "You think they send bulletins down from the big house to our shack telling us what's going on? I never knew you were coming until I saw you by the pool that day."

There was bitterness in her tone, which she usually tried to control, but with Ben she couldn't be bothered. He'd seen her at fifteen making a total fool of herself over him. Did she really care if he thought she wasn't pathetically grateful that Uncle Duncan had put a roof over her and her mother's heads? It wasn't like that didn't come at a price.

"I wrote a part for a certain star. Not even a big star. Kind of an up-and-comer. And all I mean by that is that when I'm writing, I cast parts in my head. It helps me solidify a character. So, I wrote this part thinking of a young actress named Vanessa Moore. Then, I stupidly told the casting director that's who I saw in the role.

When he cast her in the part, he must have told her I'd written the role specifically for her." He rolled his shoulders as though trying to push two boulders off the top of them. "Maybe I'm wrong and he didn't tell her. Doesn't matter. She went nuts, decided I could see into her deepest being and must be her soul mate.

"It was mildly creepy at first. She followed me everywhere and kept trying to get me alone. She told people on the set that we were an item. In the end I had to stay away from the shoot. Even though I was doing revisions, I stayed far away. But then she decided I had used her and spurned her. I swear to God she used those words. And she broke into my house and faked a suicide. In my bed."

"Oh, my God. Really?"

"Do you have to sound happy about it?"

She bit her lip. "Sorry, but look at this from my point of view. Makes my teenage crush seem pretty insignificant."

"Also, you were never batshit crazy."

"And that." She thought. "She didn't die, did she?"

"No, but she didn't keep quiet, either. She's still ranting to every fool who follows gossip blogs. Honestly, you'd think people had better things to do, but these crackpots started showing up at my house, and then there are those pond scum who write trash about movie stars. I needed a place to escape." He put up a hand and gestured to the pool house. "My folks are in Europe and I wouldn't go to them anyway. Too obvious. But mom remembered Duncan's pool house and she checked to see whether it was empty, and he immediately invited me to come and stay as long as I like."

"Can you work here?"

"It's quiet, apart from your infernal splashing every morning."

He glanced at her as he said it and their gazes connected. If she'd been writing a movie she'd have typed, *Wham, Pow*, like in a comic book. Because when he looked at her, that's what she felt: *pow*ed, *whamm*ed. The thought made her glance down at her hands where the sparkle of diamond reminded her why *wham* and *pow* were bad ideas.

"I'm going to disturb your quiet even more," she said. "Uncle Duncan and Aunt Millicent are throwing an engagement party for me."

He blinked. "You're engaged?"

"Yes. To Eric Van Hoffendam."

"Wow. Don't know him, but congrats." He didn't seem too upset that she was unavailable for wham and pow. He seemed relieved.

"Thanks."

"You don't seem like the engagement-party type." And so far he was the only one who had noticed.

"Yeah, well, I've changed a lot since I was fifteen." Though not about certain things.

"When is this big celebration?"

"Next Saturday night. I know you got an invitation." Because, even though the party was for her, Aunt Millicent had still made her address the invitation cards. She bet Cinderella never had to write out the invitations to her ball once she bagged her prince.

"I haven't been picking up my mail." He rubbed a hand over his eyes. "In fact, I haven't been doing much of anything apart from writing wooden female characters and gangsters who have to run lines with real guns in order to feel the part. God, when did I turn into such a hopeless hack?"

"You're not hopeless. I bet Vanessa Moore, who really does seem like a bimbo, has pissed you off so much you are having trouble writing your next female character, that's all."

"I should be more of a professional." He turned to her and frowned. "And when did you turn into GI Jane? You were pretty impressive back there, and way more authentic than Mike Konister."

"I wasn't acting."

He nodded. "Never thought anyone would see us. I'm sorry if I scared you."

Her lips twitched. "Not half as much as I scared Mike Konister." She touched her pistol, which she'd laid down on the table-top. "Ted and I got the idea that we wanted to learn to shoot. Uncle Duncan has a friend who belongs to a private club and he offered to teach us. Ted has no hand-eye coordination and he got bored quickly, but I turned out to be an excellent shot. We went every Saturday for most of one summer, and Wilt—that's the gun guy—told Duncan how good I was. He got me the Walther for Christmas one year. Figured I'd like it since it was the James Bond gun."

"Do you still shoot?"

"Sure, once a month or so." She grinned at him. "It's an excellent stress reliever."

"Wow. You could be my weapons expert."

She shook her head. "I can put you in touch with Wilt, though."

"Fantastic. How about you agree to be my script consultant then?"

"Script consultant?"

"Yes." His gaze was intent, and far too sexy for a woman who was engaged to another man. "You can teach me about women."

CHAPTER 6

*H*er mom woke her the next morning with the happy news that Millicent wanted to take them shopping. "She's buying you a dress for the engagement party, which is so nice of her."

Ashley yawned and sipped the coffee her mother had brought to her. "Why can't I buy my own dress and send her the bill?"

Melody sat down on the bed. "She wants to do this for you. Please let her."

"Fine." She sipped more coffee. Almost getting into a gun battle last night had made it hard to sleep.

"You're taking your nose stud out for the party, right?" her mother asked, glancing at her sideways.

What the hell? "No. I'm not taking my nose stud out for my own engagement party."

Her mother darted a slightly nervous glance her way, and she knew that look so well.

"What did Uncle Duncan say this time?" He was only her brother, but Melody treated him like her dad. He was rich, good for him, and he'd given them a home, also good for him, but he tried to control their lives. Somehow, even though he never came right out and said it, she never forgot that she owed her home to his charity. He liked to say in public that she was the daughter he'd never had, but in private Ashley felt like she was the result of a bad relationship he'd never approved of. Not that she blamed him for that; her birth father was an ass. But she didn't figure a little kid could be blamed for having bad taste in parents.

She felt that in marrying Eric she was, for the first time, getting his approval.

She doubted she'd be getting a fancy engagement party at the big house, complete with caterers and a champagne fountain, if she was marrying into a family whose name didn't appear in *Forbes* along with his.

"Only that he would really like it if you didn't wear it to the party. That's all."

She grit her teeth. Most of the time, when her mom gave her that look, she gave in because her mom was the one who'd take the heat from Uncle D. But this was her party.

"I like my nose stud. It's part of me. And Eric likes it. He's the one marrying me, not Uncle Duncan." *Ew*, that was a mental image she did not need in her head.

"It's only for one night," her mother wheedled.

"It will leave a big, stupid hole in my nose. That will look worse than the stud."

"We can fill it with concealer."

"No."

"Please, honey, you'll be moving out soon, and I'll be stuck here with Duncan. You know what a bully he is."

And how many times had she caved because of course she did know. Her uncle was a bully. He was convinced he knew better than everyone else and made sure he surrounded himself with people who let him go on believing it. He also believed money was power, and since he had so much of it and they had none, he was a tough guy to stand up to. Her mother had given up long ago and, for the most part, so had Ashley.

But this was her engagement party, not a social function for her uncle where she had to wear a pretty dress and say nice things. "I already compromised on the dress. I am not taking out my stud."

The dress may have been a "gift" from her aunt Millicent, but no gift from the big house came without so many strings attached that it was more like a net.

In the end, her mom agreed to lobby for the nose stud, and she agreed to let Aunt Millicent help her choose her dress. The three of them headed into town in Millicent's white Lincoln, and without any consultation of Ashley's wishes, stopped at a boutique whose front window triggered her gag reflex.

The dresses—and lady suits—were all elegant and restrained. Ashley didn't do ladylike and restrained. She liked indie, alternative, clothes designed by a person, preferably a young one, in a garage or on the beach with a sketchpad. Maybe the designer even sewed the things him- or herself. LA was littered with young, leading-edge designers and every one of them could use the money and the exposure. But to buy into what was essentially a conglomerate of fashion where she was certain each dress was designed by committee, that ate into her soul.

"Well, here we are," Millicent said, when they walked into the place. A woman approached who was obviously the manager. She looked like a former actress who had never made it, and now had to act like she was happy to help dress women like Millicent. She rushed up to them as though they might turn tail and run if she didn't hang onto them hard. She was aided by a second woman, who looked like a million other middle-aged women in LA: tall and blond with blue eyes and even white teeth, all trying to age like Christie Brinkley.

They fussed over Millicent, who was obviously a regular,

then turned to Ashley. "And you must be the bride?" the manager gushed.

"I guess so."

"Well, look around and let me know what catches your eye." Then she turned to the other women. "Isn't it exciting? I imagine you're looking for something to wear for the engagement party, too?"

Millicent looked embarrassed for a nanosecond; obviously it hadn't occurred to her that she might have to spring for a dress for Ashley's mom, too. She said, "This is Ashley's big day. But we'll browse, naturally."

Ashley headed to a rack of spring dresses so boring she thought she might doze off looking at them. Millicent came closer, "Now don't even look at the prices. As I said, this is my treat."

"Thank you," she whispered back. In truth, she could barely see the prices without a magnifying glass. This was the kind of place where if you had to ask the price you couldn't afford it. She didn't even want to afford it.

She was staring at a black dress that had a silver zipper running up the front and some kind of metallic band on the bottom. She thought maybe she could do something with that if she wore boots and went heavy on the eye makeup when Millicent gently but firmly turned her away. "No black on your engagement party, sweetheart." And she was led back to the 'appropriate' area. In the end, she gave up. What was the point in struggling against the inevitable?"

The dress that Millicent chose—with the help of the manager and the manager's assistant—and the dress she hated the least, was a silk underdress in pink topped with a chiffon overdress that looked as though dozens of flower blossoms had fluttered down and stuck to it. The skirt was full and flowing.

Wearing it, she felt as though she were putting on a costume to play a part. Naturally, the torture didn't end until she also owned a pair of heels to match. As she stood looking at herself in the triple mirror, she thought, God, the only thing missing is a string of pearls.

As though she'd darted the thought out of her brain and straight into Millicent's like a deviant paper airplane, Millicent piped up, "Oh, I have the perfect string of pearls. I'll lend them to you."

As she opened her mouth to reject the offer, her mom piped up, "Not the pearls Duncan bought you in Paris?"

Millicent patted her on the shoulder. "Ashley's my niece."

Her mom, obviously realizing Ashley had no idea what was so special about these pearls, said, "Those pearls belonged to Wallis Simpson, you know, the American who married Edward VIII. Well, except he never got to be king. He chose her instead."

Great. She'd be wearing the pearls of a woman who took the throne away from a king. Also, if her history was correct, the woman had been a Nazi sympathizer. Exactly the sort of person whose pearls a girl wanted to wear to her engagement party.

She knew from the unspoken communication coming from her mother as loud as shouting that she was to take the damned pearls and be grateful. And, frankly, how much worse could this outfit be? Though if anyone mentioned white gloves she'd lose it.

Luckily, no one did. She said, thank you, to her aunt and they left with a box and a huge bag. The bag was pale green with a curly logo in gold.

As they stepped out, she felt like there should be a driver waiting for them who'd pile the boxes and bags into the car and drive them to lunch. But lunch was obviously not part of the plan. Millicent drove them home and dropped them at the cottage, and she said her polite thanks once more.

When they got into the cottage, she said, "Mom, how could you let her stick me with this dress?"

"It's a beautiful dress," her mom protested.

She gave her the evil eye.

Her mom sighed, and walked to the kitchen where she poured them both a glass of water. "They do a lot for us, and they're excited to be putting on this party for you. Does it really matter? Most of the people there will be Duncan and Millicent's friends and the Van Hoffendams' friends. When you go out to party with your own friends you can wear whatever you like."

"I guess," but it still felt wrong to dress like another person to make her aunt and uncle happy. Shouldn't they be happy with who she was?

Like that had ever happened.

"I think me marrying Eric is the first thing I've ever done that makes Uncle Duncan happy."

Her mom made a face. "He's happy one of us is getting married."

"You ask me, this is about Ted and Kate breaking up." She'd thought a lot about why her aunt and uncle were so excited about this wedding. The only explanation that made sense to her was that this was a way to save face in front of their stuffy friends after their own son had broken off his engagement a couple of weeks before the big day.

"Maybe a little bit." Her mom turned to her. "But isn't it nice to actually be treated like somebody for a change?"

But she wasn't finished dishing about Ted. "I always thought he was a mini-me version of his Dad, but secretly he was in love with a woman who'd been a stripper, or hooker or something."

Her mom nodded. "Very *Pretty Woman*."

"Whatever. Is he coming to the engagement party?"

"I don't know. I'm not sure if he and Duncan are even on speaking terms yet."

"Kind of awkward when they work together in the family company."

"I know. But can I be a real bitch for a minute and say how nice it is not to have Perfect Ted held up as the model child?"

"Makes your hell babe a little more acceptable, huh?"

"You're not my hell babe. You're untraditional. Like me."

And look how that had turned out.

"I hope he comes, and I hope he brings the stripper-hooker."

"He'd never do that."

"Maybe he'll see me in Wallis Simpson's pearls and tear them from my throat, demanding them for his bride."

"An appropriate woman to wear them."

"Unlike me." She couldn't work up the energy for the full evil eye, so she made do with a frown.

Her mom slugged down water like it was a tequila shot. Maybe she wished it was. "Look, Ash, you must know the bride's parents are supposed to pay for the wedding. I don't have the money to pay for it. Not to the standard the Van Hoffendams want. They said they'd pay, but I don't want their charity. Millicent hinted pretty strongly that she and Duncan would help with the costs." She shrugged. "You're their niece... I'd rather take their money."

"But I don't care about a big wedding. I don't even want one. Neither does Eric."

Her mother gave her a look that suggested she was still a child. "When the Carnarvons and the Van Hoffendams merge, trust me, there's going to be a big wedding."

"Even if the bride and groom don't want one? What is this, the middle ages?"

"Pretty much. Come on, be practical for once. I never was. Learn from my mistakes. If you let them throw you a nice wedding it will make them happy, and it will make the Van Hoffendams happy. You'll have a great party and your lives together will get off to the right start."

"Plus, they can tell the caterers to thaw all the food they had prepared for Ted's wedding."

Her mother gulped more water in that disturbing tequila-shot manner of hers. "There will be lots of really expensive gifts, things you couldn't afford just starting out. You've seen Cinderella. This could be your ticket out of the servants' quarters."

She smiled. "Eric's not much of a prince charming, though." She couldn't imagine him running around chasing after her because she lost a shoe.

"But you love him, right?" Strangely, no one had asked her that.

"I guess so. We've known each other long enough. It's not like there are a lot of surprises. I was pretty shocked when he proposed, though, to be honest. But it makes sense. Our friends are getting married and he's thinking about getting a real job."

"Define thinking about."

With his terrible high school marks, not even his legacy status or his family money and connections could get Eric a spot at the family's traditional Ivy League school. He'd ended up at USC and barely scraped through. She'd helped him with his English papers and read his textbooks so she could help him study. He'd always said he got his degree so his parents would shut up about it. Of course, now that he was finished college, they were pressuring him about a job. She wondered if getting married was a way of diverting attention from his job search.

"He's going to take the stock broker's course."

"Really? Is he interested in stocks?"

In fact, he'd told her it was easy money and he planned to spend most of his time wining and dining clients while the really smart people figured out what stocks and things he should recommend. "Yeah, he's interested in business."

"That's good. Some men take a little longer to get serious about life."

"I guess." She was still fretting about the wedding. "I never thought about the actual wedding when he asked me. I thought we could go to city hall or something to get married, then get a few friends together and a keg of beer and party."

"After you're married you can have keg parties if you still want them. Trust me on this, you'll only waste your energy and get a headache if you try and stop the Carnarvons and the Van Hoffendams. They're like the Hatfields and the McCoys, only on the same side."

"Scary."

"Come on. Let's put on clothes we actually like and go grab a burger somewhere, just the two of us."

She knew when her mom tried to have a *Gilmore Girls* moment that she was trying to apologize. "Sure. That would be fun."

Even though she had a Spanish test to study for. But she was a quick study, always had been.

CHAPTER 7

*I*t was the night of her engagement party and the grounds and gardens of the Carnarvon estate looked as pretty as Ashley had ever seen them. Candlelit lanterns hung from trees and twinkle lights sparkled. There were two outdoor bars set up as well as two inside the house, and uniformed waiters in tuxedos and white gloves paraded along the twining paths offering trays of champagne, and more trays of exquisite appetizers. She had been to parties that her aunt and uncle organized before, she'd even served at a few, but this party was actually for her. For her!

Maybe her dress was more traditional than she would have chosen, but she was here, engaged to an amazing, fun-loving guy, and she'd won the nose-stud argument.

People who had never taken any notice of her before were making a point of coming up and congratulating her, offering her smooth, scented cheeks to be kissed. Eric looked like a prince from a fairytale, his blonde hair glowing in the moonlight like old gold. He had trimmed his beard and put on a tuxedo she hadn't realized he owned. When he gazed at her, she felt like they were sharing a secret joke. Like it was them against the world.

He took her hand loosely in his. "You look beautiful."

She grinned at him. "Thanks. I feel like I'm playing dress-up in my mother's clothes, but at least I got to keep my nose stud."

He leaned in. "I would never have recognized you without it."

There were plenty of business acquaintances of both the Carnarvons and the Van Hoffendams, but there were also plenty of Ashley and Eric's friends. Whitney and Bradley arrived and Whitney whispered to Ashley that Bradley hadn't wanted to come. He was terrified she'd put pressure on him to get married.

Sienna arrived with her parents, who were friends of the Carnarvons. "Great party," she said, scooping a glass of champagne off a tray. "Anybody interesting and single here?"

She glanced around. "Over sixty or under?"

"After a few more of these I probably won't care."

Melissa and Douglas were there, holding hands as though their palms had been welded together and to ever separate them would cause permanent damage. They were getting married next summer. Melissa said, "I am so happy to have someone else to go through this with. Isn't being engaged the best?"

She pinned a bright smile on her face. "Absolutely."

Donovan and Kylie arrived soon after. Both squealed when they saw her and ran over to give her hugs. Kylie said, "I can't believe you and Eric are getting married. I didn't even know you were going out! I thought you were like, you know, friends with benefits." Coming from another woman those words could have been considered catty. But Kylie was one of those people who blurted out whatever she was thinking. She was impossible not to like. "I'm crazy about Eric," she said, glancing toward where he was standing in front of the closest bar joking with some of his cronies.

"Who wouldn't be? He's gorgeous and rich," Sienna said. "Nobody ever thought he'd settle down."

Melissa glanced significantly down at her stomach. "You're not..." She waved a hand up and down her own abdomen. "You know."

Ashley's face wrinkled in horror. "Pregnant? No. I should change my Facebook status to *Not Pregnant*."

"You should at least change it to *In a Relationship*."

"I know, I keep forgetting." In fact, she was waiting for Eric to change his.

Melissa was still looking at her strangely. "It's just that we saw you and Eric at a party on, what, Friday? And then Tuesday, there was an engagement announcement in all the papers. It seemed kind of rushed, like maybe there was a reason?"

"I promise you I am not pregnant. I think the Van Hoffendams are just super organized people. Honestly, they practically had the entire wedding figured out at our first dinner together."

"I wish they'd plan *my* wedding," Kylie said. "The wedding coordinator is a nightmare. Honestly, she wants everything her way. Like she knows best, or something." She blew out a breath. "Next time I get married, I'm eloping."

Sienna laughed. "And only in LA does that line sound normal."

Melissa said, "I totally think the three of us should have a joint bachelorette party. How fun would that be?"

She giggled, "Amazing." Especially since Whitney and Sienna hadn't got around to organizing anything. She loved those girls, but she suspecting downloading the wedding planner app was as much as they'd manage to do.

"My dad says we can use his boat; we could go on a harbor cruise! He'd crew the boat, and send over his personal chef to make dinner. Of course there's a full bar, and then we can go clubbing somewhere. What do you think?"

"Yeah, sure. I guess."

"So? Have you got a venue yet?"

"I think we'll probably have the wedding here."

"Yeah. This place is amazing. How about your dress? Have you picked anything out yet?"

She could not tell these legitimately rich girls that she was going to be wearing a hand-me-down, so she said, "I've been looking but I haven't completely decided yet. How about you?"

Melissa's pretty face drooped into a frown. She lowered her tone, "Okay, you can't tell anyone this, but my mother phoned Evangeline. You know, the one who designs the gowns for all the celebrities? She got me an interview. I have never been so scared. I spent the whole day in the salon getting my hair done, a facial, manicure, pedicure, make-up professionally applied. The works. I even had some kind of body wrap that was supposed to sweat off pounds.

"And when I got to her studio, after making us wait for half an hour, Evangeline had me stand in front of her and turn around in a circle then walk up and down. And then she said, 'Call me when you lose 10 pounds and we'll talk.'"

"My God, she did not."

Melissa nodded, "She totally did. Now, on top of the stress of the wedding, I'm on a diet." She screwed up her face. "I hate dieting. It has the opposite effect on me. All I do is think about food all the time. I've gained two pounds since I saw Evangeline."

She tried not to laugh. Melissa had always been on the plump side but it suited her. "Get another dress. Douglas loves you the way you are. He doesn't care if you wear an Evangeline gown."

"I know, you're right. It's more my mother's dream than mine anyway. She wants the bragging rights," she sighed. "You look great by the way. Nice pearls."

"Thanks." Ashley thought that Wallis Simpson must have had

a much smaller neck than she did since the pearls felt as though they were choking her. But, she knew how much Millicent was enjoying the evening.

Ashley mingled. She made polite small talk with people she barely knew and spent time with her own friends. Eric spent more time at the bar than by her side, but she was used to that.

She stood there, in this fairytale garden, in a dress that seemed to float around her when she moved, and glanced down one of the candlelit paths. A man stepped out of the shadows and moved toward her. For a moment her heart skipped a beat. He seemed like he'd appeared out of nowhere, a mysterious and fascinating figure, and then he stepped into the light and she recognized Ben. He wore a crisp dark suit, and his hair was neater than she'd ever seen it, but his eyes caught hers and burned like a wild animal's in the jungle. He stepped toward her and she stood there waiting for him. When her heart bumped her ribs and Wallis's pearls felt like fingers squeezing her throat, she realized that her teenage crush wasn't completely gone. He still affected her.

"You're late." She put her hands on her hips and tilted her head. "Trouble finding the place?"

"Wasn't sure I'd make it at all. I was in meetings."

"No problem. Everything okay?"

"Yeah, everything will be. You look great by the way. Congratulations."

"On looking great or getting married?"

"Both, I guess."

She put a hand to his sleeve and her engagement ring winked. "Come on, I'll introduce you around, and let's find you a drink."

For a moment he resisted the pull on his arm. "Don't introduce me. I only came to see you and to make an appearance for Duncan and Millicent."

"Right. I forgot that you're hiding out here. If anyone asks who you are I'll just say you're an international man of mystery."

"If you weren't wearing a pretty dress I'd throw you in the pool right now."

She snorted. "You'd be doing me a favor."

"Cinderella doesn't like her ball gown?"

"I feel like I'm playing dress-up."

"Those are some very nice pearls." She had no idea if he made a habit of studying pearls or whether he was making fun of her, but she suspected the latter.

"Thank you. They were last worn by a woman who pulled a king off his throne."

"She's an amateur compared to you."

She raised her brows, giving him a silent, *What?*

"She wasn't a trained marksman like yourself. You'd have put a bullet through his heart."

"Well, wouldn't have, but could have."

"Don't underestimate yourself."

Their gazes connected and she experienced one of those topsy-turvy moments where she wondered, is he attracted, or is he only teasing? And how she wished he'd shown a millionth of this much interest in her when she was a teenager and would have loved it. "I'll try not to."

He looked as though he were going to say something when she heard Grace Van Hoffendam calling her name. "Ashley, there you are. I've been looking all over for you." At her side was a very pretty blonde woman about Ashley's age. Someone she was sure she'd never met. They did the half smile thing, while Grace glanced significantly at Bennett. He'd said he didn't want to be introduced, but what choice did she have? She stuck to, "Grace, this is Ben, he's a family friend."

She didn't tell her future mother-in-law that Ben was one of the hottest young male writers in the country or that he was living in a pool house on the property.

"Nice to meet you," he said. Then, obviously realizing Grace wanted him gone, he added, "Excuse me. I need to go and find Duncan."

Grace smiled regally at him. "I just left him. He's in the conservatory discussing grain futures with my husband."

"Thanks," Ben said, and strode off as though he couldn't wait to get the inside scoop on the grain business.

When he was out of sight, her future mother-in-law stepped closer. "Ashley," Grace said, smiling her most winning smile, "I have such a favor to ask of you. This is Tasmine."

The blonde smiled, a smile that would make an orthodontist proud, so straight and white were her teeth. "Like Jasmine, with a T."

"Got it."

"Tasmine is a cousin of Eric's and it would mean so much to our family if you would consider inviting her to be a bridesmaid. She's been a bridesmaid at quite a few other weddings and she's a very experienced planner."

"Wow," Ashley said, feeling completely trapped, as Grace must've known she'd feel when she made the request right in front of Blondie. "I've already chosen my bridesmaids."

"Well, if you could squeeze in one more, I so hope you'll consider including Tasmine." She smiled at the pair of them as though it were done deal. "Now, I'll leave you two to get acquainted."

After Grace moved away, there was a moment's awkward silence. Tasmine broke it. "I'm sorry, I know Grace can be a little forceful, but I'd really love to be involved if I could be of any help at all. Eric and I used to play together when we were little, and it would mean a lot to me to be a part of his wedding."

"I'm not trying to be rude, but I've known Eric for more than ten years and he's never mentioned you."

Tasmine didn't seem insulted. Or even surprised. She laughed. "Eric was always more memorable than I was, even when he was a little boy. My family moved away when I was eleven, but you never really forget your first crush."

Behind Tasmine she saw Ben sip something that looked like a gin and tonic while he chatted politely with Millicent. "No, you never do forget your first."

"Well, what do you think? Am I a contender?"

If nothing else, she liked Tasmine's clear communication, so she tried some of her own. "How many times have you been a bridesmaid?"

The woman tilted her head as though thinking deeply. "Ten. No, eleven."

"Wow, you really are experienced. So, would you be any good at, say, running interference between me and my future mother-in-law?"

"See, here's what's so great about me as a bridesmaid. I can be the one who tells Grace to," she paused for a second to glance right and left and then lowered her voice, "let's say, back off, if she gets a little too involved in the planning."

"You could do that?"

"Absolutely. I feel that it is the job of the bridesmaid to make certain that the bride's life runs smoothly up to and including the wedding day. I don't have to be part of Van Hoffendams' immediate family after the wedding, but you do. So, it makes perfect sense for me to be the bad guy, assuming of course that a bad guy is necessary."

"How many times have you had to play bad guy in one of your weddings?"

Those big blue eyes twinkled at her. "Ten. No, eleven."

Ashley couldn't help but laugh. "You sound like the perfect bridesmaid." Whitney and Sienna had been happy to be asked, but they'd never offered their services as guardians. She kind of liked the notion. "What else would you do?" She had never thought before of bridesmaids as being anything but her closest friends who got to stand up with her on the big day. The idea of a bridesmaid who actually did something useful was novel and quite exciting.

"Oh, lots of things. At the last wedding where I was a bridesmaid, we had a lot of people with food allergies. It was a strangely allergic family. I took on the job of liaising with the caterer. Let's see, I also coordinated all the bridesmaids' schedules so that we could shop for bridesmaid dresses together, and then I made sure that the dresses were all finished on time and all delivered to the correct bridesmaids. I also organized the bachelorette night." She flipped her hair over her shoulder. "As you can see, I like to organize things. To me it's not work, it's fun."

As much as it irked Ashley that Grace had put her in such an awkward position by asking her to include Tasmine in the wedding party right in front of her, she had to admit Eric's childhood playmate sounded like a dream bridesmaid. "You're not one of those people who comes across as really nice and then turns psycho are you?"

"I don't think so. I could give you the phone numbers of some of the brides I've stood up for, I'm sure they'd vouch for me." Then her eyes lit up. "Oh, there's Eric. I haven't seen him in so long. Do you mind if I go and say hi?"

CHAPTER 8

*B*en was accustomed to fantasy. He worked in the movie business after all. But he'd rarely experienced such a feeling of unreality as he did at Ashley Carnarvon's engagement party. He couldn't put his finger on why, but the entire event felt staged. More than simply staged in the sense of hiring a caterer to prepare foods no one usually ate, or dressing in uncomfortable clothes, or putting a load of candles up in the trees. There was an undercurrent of unreality.

The whole thing fascinated him, and so he stayed longer than he'd planned. Also, he realized he'd been working too hard lately with too few breaks and it was probably good for him to mix with other humans.

He chatted with Millicent over a drink, and then, since Duncan had last been seen in the conservatory, followed a line of twinkling lights around a secluded path. He'd made an appearance tonight mostly out of respect for Duncan and Millicent Carnarvon who had been nice enough to let him stay on the property and hide out. He also wanted to cheer Ashley on and get an idea of the man she was marrying.

He entered the conservatory and was struck, as always in

such places, by the smell of wet earth. As soon as he got all the way inside, his skin felt sticky with humidity. There was no one in there as far as he could tell. He wondered if Grace Carnarvon had told him he'd find Duncan in the conservatory just to get rid of him. But, as soon as he took a couple of steps inside, skirting around a profusion of blooming orchids, he heard low male voices and recognized one of them as Duncan's. Grain futures was a serious business, he realized, as he heard the note of fierceness in Duncan's tone. Then he made out the words and frowned.

"Judge Bailey had better drop all charges—and completely—or this deal is off."

"I can assure you that all the arrangements have been made. You've got absolutely nothing to worry about."

"This is my family. Nobody messes with my family."

A hint of irritation entered the voice of the other man, whom he assumed was Charles Van Hoffendam. "She'd never have achieved a match like this if it weren't for these extraordinary circumstances. Trust me, nobody messes with my family either. This is a case of you and me helping each other and our families. Let's be honest here, we'll both profit."

There was silence for a moment. Ben stood completely still, knowing he'd walked in on something that was nothing to do with the stock markets and not quite knowing how to leave without drawing attention to himself. He heard a scraping sound that he thought might be one of the men, Duncan probably, adjusting the location of a flowerpot. Neither Duncan nor Millicent spent much time in this conservatory as far as he could see. It seemed like they hired someone to potter around with their orchids and their exotic plants as they hired people to do all the other mundane tasks in their lives.

He felt that Duncan was moving the pot around to give himself something to do. At last Duncan said, "All right. I trust you to take care of this efficiently and quietly. And that there will be no further incidents in the future."

"Of course."

"What about the papers? The media?"

"Don't you worry about that. It's under control."

In the dim light he saw the men shake hands. "Well, I suppose we'd better get back to our guests. You know, we've offered to pay for this wedding. Melody is a very nice woman and of course she wants to do the right thing for her daughter, but, well, we have a quality to the way we do things. Our guests, some of whom are my business associates, have certain standards that must be upheld."

The two men began heading back into the house through an inside door so Ben was able to remain in his spot undetected. He wasn't particularly interested in eavesdropping, but he felt that everyone would be embarrassed if he made his presence known, so he took the easy route and stood silent. As the two men left he heard Duncan say, with a hint of sarcasm, "I think you've got enough expenses on your hands. Don't worry, Millicent and I will take care of the wedding costs. We never had a daughter. Ashley's as close as we'll ever come. We're happy to help her get started in life." Then his lofty tone changed to one of contempt. "And God knows her mother hasn't got two cents to rub together."

"And the father?" Charles Van Hoffendam asked after a moment.

"Not in the picture," he answered shortly.

He heard the door open to the main house and then close behind the two men, and he heard no more.

Wow. That had been an interesting conversation. He wasn't completely sure what he'd overheard, but the entire content of it made him uneasy. What did Judge Bailey have to do with anything? The judge was an old family friend of the Carnarvons and of his family's, too. He'd assumed he'd see the man here tonight, had looked forward to it in the way he enjoyed seeing his parents' friends in small doses.

Duncan Carnarvon and the man he assumed was Eric Van Hoffendam's father had talked as though this wedding was a business deal. They'd even mentioned the word profit, as well as keeping something out of the media. As a current media target himself, that was something he'd love to be able to do.

His mind was racing as he reversed his steps and exited the conservatory the same way he'd come in. He took a detour, returning from the direction of the beach so if anyone saw him they'd never guess where he'd been.

The few minutes' walk allowed him to process the unusual conversation between the two men. Naturally, since he was a storyteller, he began to weave possibilities. Most of which were completely preposterous, which was typical of real life. So many things that happened in life would never sell as a screenplay since they were too improbable. Sometimes he felt that movies were closer to reality than reality was.

As he strode up the path that led by the beach, he passed in front of the cottage where Ashley and her mother lived. He was thrown back in time for a second, remembering how, when he was walking down to the beach to surf, he had to pass what was clearly her bedroom. He soon discovered she was on the watch for him, for no sooner would he pass her window than he'd hear the sound of a sash window being dragged open. Next thing he knew, she'd be scrambling to catch up, trying to act cool, sauntering down to the beach as though it were coincidence that they were going to the water at the same time.

Maybe it was the memory of that achingly vulnerable young girl and her crush on him, but he felt a genuine fondness for her. Sure, she was grown up now, and certainly seemed as though she could handle herself and was long over her feelings for him. But he'd still look out for her if he could. Besides, his curiosity was whetted. Not only to find out whether Judge

Bailey was at the party tonight, but he was now also determined to spend a few minutes getting to know the bridegroom.

When he drew close to the big house, he scanned the area looking for the judge, but it was impossible to pick one person out. There were groups of people standing in clusters outside, guests streaming in and out of the open doors. He could spend all night looking and never find the object of his search.

He soon spotted Millicent and knew she'd save him the trouble. He walked up to her, "What a great party," he said.

She gave him a practiced hostess smile. "I'm so glad you're enjoying it. Have you had something to eat? There's a full spread laid out in the dining room."

"Great. I was hoping to see Judge Bailey. I'm sure he's here, being as he's such an old family friend, but I can't find him."

She dropped her hostess mask for a second. "I absolutely expected him to come. He's Ted's godfather, practically part of the family. But he sent his regrets. Apparently, a weekend trip with his wife to New York was more important."

"Maybe there's a ballet or something. You know they never miss the premieres."

"Well, if there is, this is the first I've heard of it." Then she switched back into hostess mode. "Let me introduce you to a few people. Not that we socialize with any movie people, but you never know when connections will come in handy."

"That's really nice of you," he said, already taking a step backward, "but I'm keeping a low profile. I only dropped by to wish Ashley well and say hello to you and Duncan."

"That's so nice of you. And how are your parents doing?"

"Great, I talked with mother yesterday. They're in Paris but heading to Italy, and then thinking of spending a few days in Prague before they come home."

"Wonderful. Give her my love next time you talk to her."

"I will. And now, I think I'll check out that buffet."

He headed inside and found his way to the dining room. As

he'd suspected, the long table was loaded with food and uniformed caterers served everything from wafer thin smoked salmon to slices of beef, salads, and little tiny things that looked too fancy to eat. He loaded his plate, since he had been more interested in writing than in cooking for himself recently, and he spent a few minutes talking to a hot redhead who was as happy to flirt with him as he was to flirt with her. Not that anything could come of it, he reminded himself. Lester had been pretty clear. No girls for poor Ben. Not until Vanessa had some new victim on the line.

After he'd polished off a second plate of amazing food, he stopped by the bar, thinking he'd enjoy a scotch before calling it a night and heading back to his computer and the scene that wouldn't come together for him.

A group of young guys around Ashley's age congregated around the bar, joking and acting like fools. He'd probably been that much of a tool himself half a decade ago, but he hoped not.

The center of the group was a blond-haired dude with a stupid grin on his face and heavy-lidded eyes, possibly from drink.

"Can't believe you're getting shackled, man," another semi-drunk guy said to the blond fellow. His interest sharpened. This must be the famous Eric.

"I know."

"You knock her up or something?"

He shook his head, leaning back against a tree as though he were posing for a menswear ad.

"It's not one of your jokes, is it?" the guy glanced around and a grin spread over his face. "'Cause it would be a good one. Having the Carnarvons lay on this spread and be like, hey, *punked*, only kidding."

Ben felt heat start to rise up the back of his neck. Ashley Carnarvon was ten times better than any of these pricks currently trying to figure out why some self-satisfied little piss-ant might want to marry her.

"Ashley's a great girl," Eric said. "It's not a joke."

"Anyway, I don't know how you're going to top the last prank."

Those lazy eyes opened fully and Ben stepped forward to order his scotch as though he hadn't been eavesdropping, which was becoming a bad habit tonight.

Eric glanced at him briefly, then said, "Toad, I need to talk to you." He glanced at Ben. "Let's go inside. You too, Slade."

The two chosen ones trotted behind the guy he was pretty sure was Eric Van Hoffendam. They'd left one guy behind and Ben saw him looking after the retreating trio. He looked a little younger than the others. If he was a dog, his tail would be drooping.

The bartender served up his scotch in a heavy tumbler. No plastic glasses at this outdoor party. He sidled up to the lost pup. "That Eric's quite the practical joker, huh?" he asked.

A low chuckle answered him. "Oh, yeah. He's famous for them. And most of the time you never see them coming."

He sipped his drink. Just two guys hanging out, shooting the breeze. "He ever get you?"

"Not really, but one time he got my older brother Todd. That's the guy he calls Toad. He talked Toad and Slade and their other buddies into streaking during the school principal's opening address at high school their senior year. He totally acted like he was going to do it too, so they all ran naked in front of the principal while Eric filmed them."

"So, they got busted and he got away with it?" What a prince.

"Naah, he totally admitted it. They all got suspended for two days. Oh, and there was another time when he put vodka in all the water bottles for the football team. Every one of them. Course, these guys gulped half the bottle down before they realized."

Ben pretended to be amused. "So, I guess your team won, huh?"

"No, see, that's what's so great about his pranks. He put the vodka in both teams' water bottles. He didn't care who won, he just wanted to watch them play loaded. Funniest thing you've ever seen. It's probably still on YouTube."

"So, you think he got engaged to the Carnarvon girl as a joke?"

He shook his head. "Only my brother would think that, because he's stupid. There's nothing funny about getting engaged to someone for a joke. That's mean."

"And his jokes aren't mean?"

"Not usually. Mainly he does things when he's bored."

"He do anything really good recently?"

Again, Toad's younger brother shook his head. "I don't know. I think something happened a couple weeks ago, but Toad was so hung over the next day he couldn't even talk. Then I went back to college."

They chatted for a few minutes about the kid's school and then he excused himself to go talk to someone else.

He circulated, chatting more than he'd expected to, and enjoying himself a lot more than he'd imagined he would. But all the time his mind was whirring. He tried to keep one eye on Ashley and one on her fiancé. What he noted was that he barely saw them together. Hardly the most encouraging sign in a newly engaged pair at the party celebrating their engagement.

She wasn't staring wistfully after Eric, either. Not like that inseparable pair, was it Donovan and Rylie? Kylie? Something like that. When Donovan went to the bathroom, Rylie/Kylie stared after him until he returned to clasp her hand in his once more.

Ashley seemed perfectly happy hanging out with her girl-friends, mingling with whoever all these people were. Showing off a ring that to his eye was the diamond ring equivalent of beige. Who would choose the world's most ubiquitous style of engagement ring for a woman whose charm was her quirkiness?

Were they trying to turn her into one of them?

He gazed at her, in the dress that was way too conservative and the ring that was *way* too conservative and had to wonder. Was she going to let them?

He got a chance to see more of the groom when Duncan called everyone together so he could propose a toast. "Eric?" he called out in his commanding, booming tones. "Ashley?" He glanced around and plastered a big grin on his face. "Come on over here, kids."

Ashley arrived first, looking a little embarrassed but smiling at the assembled guests as though being called out to listen to Duncan drone on was the highlight of her evening.

Eric von Hoffendam arrived almost a minute later, shuffling up, with his shoulders slumped, looking more like an overgrown kid who was in trouble than a man celebrating his engagement to the love of his life. He gazed around at the assembled crowd, all smiling and nodding at him and Ashley, and, as though it was an afterthought put an arm around her.

Duncan Carnarvon made a speech. There was nothing unusual about this; Duncan Carnarvon was wont to give speeches and Ben had heard plenty of them. He gave them at the office and at fundraisers and the odd political event. He talked about his niece and how he'd known her since she was a child, watched her grow into a lovely young woman, *blah blah blah*, and then said how very happy he was that she had found her partner.

He then indulged his captive audience in the story of how he had met his wife Millicent and how lucky he was, and that he hoped Ashley and Eric would be as happy as Duncan and Millicent had been all these years. And then, finally, he proposed a toast to the engaged couple.

Ben raised his glass along with everyone else, and while they politely chorused, "To the engaged couple," he looked at Ashley and mumbled, "What the hell are you thinking?"

He didn't stay much longer after that. He had work to do.

IN THE LAST FEW WEEKS, since his life had become a joke and Vanessa Moore came up with a new punch line every time he thought the laughter had ended, Ben had discovered that writing a really violent, morally ambivalent crime drama was very good therapy. And in this therapy, he got paid.

But when he got back to the pool house, strangely he could not focus. He flipped on his computer but the scenes wouldn't take shape. He'd only had two drinks, so it wasn't alcohol messing with his mind. It was something else. Through the open louvers he could hear the party still going on, though he could tell that it was winding down.

He wasn't a smoker, but he allowed himself a rare cigar. Tonight, he felt as though he could use his occasional indulgence. He headed outside and sat on one of the lounge chairs at the edge of the pool. He liked it here, quiet and out of the way. The pool sparkled like a blue topaz that some giantess might wear on her hand. Even though the engagement party was on the same property, it seemed miles away. The twinkling lights and bursts of laughter could be coming from another planet. He puffed his cigar and settled back, gazing up into the blue, blue heavens. And then it hit him. The reason he had this uncomfortable feeling in his gut had nothing to do with whatever secrets Duncan Carnarvon and Charles Van Hoffendam had been swapping.

His unease was about Ashley's choice of husband. He hadn't disliked Eric, but he hadn't liked him either. Most of all, he didn't like him with Ashley. He'd seemed dismissive of her, too busy laughing with his friends and drinking more than was good for him to pay attention to the woman he was going to marry. If he was this useless a partner at his engagement party, what kind of a husband was he going to be?

Not that it was any of Ben's business. He was simply an observer, a storyteller.

*a*shley might love her secret vision of herself as a rebel, but she had grown up on the Carnarvon estate and her social manners were as ingrained as her DNA. She circulated, she made nice. But inside she grew increasingly irked that Eric was spending more time with his buddies than he was with her. As the night progressed, she went from irked to downright pissed. And speaking of pissed, she had a feeling, as the hour closed in on midnight, that if her husband-to-be weren't leaning against the trunk of the tree outside on the big patio where the bar was set up, he'd fall flat on his face.

She walked over to where Eric was hunkered down with his buddies and he didn't look as though he was budging anytime soon. "Hi," she said.

He turned to look at her lazily. "Ash, hey. Come have a drink."

His friend Toad piped up, "Hey, Ash. Great party."

"Thanks."

She pinned a tight smile to her face. "Eric? Can I talk to you for a sec?"

"Yeah, sure."

She waited but he remained where he was. As though the tree might fall down if he didn't hold it up. His gaze was fixed on her face, waiting for her to speak. "Um, I meant privately."

"Oh. Okay." He pushed away from the tree and after a small wobble, managed to walk over to where she was. She took a few more steps so they had relative privacy.

He came closer, ran a finger under the scoop of pearls. "So, you coming over to my place later?"

"I was thinking maybe we'd leave together."

"But my friends are all here."

"This is *our* engagement party." She voiced each word slowly so they'd sink in.

"Yeah, so?"

"So, maybe you should spend some more time with me. I've been totally humiliated tonight. You spent more time with your hooligan friends than with me."

He blinked, as though she'd attacked him for no reason. "But I always hang out with my friends. And you hang out with yours. That's how it works. Then we hook up later."

How could he be so dense? "But we're engaged."

"So?"

"So, you're not acting like a fiancé."

He looked down his Van Hoffendam nose at her, a nose that had been bred over generations for looking down from. "Which is weird, since you're already acting like a nagging wife."

Then he turned away and swaggered back to his friends. She stood there, feeling stunned and foolish, and heard a burst of hearty male laughter. She had no idea what they were laughing at but she had a deep suspicion Eric had made some crack about her, marriage, women, or a combination of all those things.

She stood where she was for a few more minutes and then decided that if Eric didn't want to leave with her, she'd leave by herself. And she'd walk herself all the way home, to the cottage. Eric could go screw himself.

She found Millicent and discreetly returned the pearls to their rightful owner. "Thank you for lending them to me."

Millicent patted her cheek fondly. "They looked lovely with that dress. And one day, these will belong to you anyway."

Ashley smiled and tried to look delighted, though in fact she felt as though the name choker was an apt one. No matter how she tried to rearrange the marble-sized pearls, there had always been one poking her in the larynx.

Melody was hunkered down in the big dining room with a group of her own friends, chowing down on the remains of that sumptuous meal. Uncle Duncan was holding forth with his cronies and a bottle of scotch she suspected was both very old and very expensive. Everyone, in fact, seemed to be having more fun than she was.

But, the moon was full, the grounds were pretty and the smell of night blooming jasmine permeated the air. Her skin began to tingle. Her steps led her almost without her own volition to the swimming pool. She hadn't enjoyed a midnight swim in a while. Ben had left the party early, and with luck he was sound asleep in bed so she could indulge herself. She could throw off the clothes that didn't feel like hers and dive into the pool. She slipped off her silver heels as she drew closer and walked barefoot to the edge of the pool. She stared into its welcoming depth and the tingle on her skin was interrupted by a prickle of awareness.

She raised her head and realized she could smell a hint of cigar smoke. She glanced around and there he was. At his ease in a lounger, shirt open at the neck and legs crossed casually at the ankle. "Don't let me stop you," he said. "It's a nice night for swim."

Well, he had caught her now. There was no point pretending she hadn't come here to swim, when he saw her do it almost every day. "It is a nice night. I came by to dip my feet in the water and cool them down." She suited her action to her words and dipped one throbbing foot into the deliciously cool water. "I hate wearing heels."

"What happened to the fancy jewels?"

She was puzzled. "My what?"

He made a swinging motion under his chin. "Your royalty-toppling pearls."

"Oh, those." She dipped her other foot in the water and swished it around a little. "I had to give them back."

Even in the dim moonlight she could see the amusement cross his face. "Let's see, your jewels had to be returned, you've left the party with no shoes on. Does that dress disappear at midnight?"

"No, I'm hanging on to the dress."

"Only because I was a gentleman and let you know I was watching. You were this close to dropping your laundry and diving into that pool."

He rose and stepped slowly toward her. She felt her heart rate speed up. She wanted to turn tail and run but she didn't. She stood her ground and watched him approach. "I–" What was the point in denying it? They both knew she'd planned to ditch her dress and dive in.

He was close now. So close she could see the wrinkles in his dress shirt from where he'd been sitting down. "Only thing is, I don't see a bathing suit."

His words were like warm fingers stroking her skin. Crazy to feel such a reaction but she couldn't seem to prevent her body from acting as though she were still the love struck fool she'd been at fifteen.

"I…I must have forgotten it." Oh, brilliant. Exactly the witty, sexy comeback he was used to from the movies.

He didn't seem to care that she wasn't a master of sparkling dialogue. He seemed perfectly happy to stand way inside her personal space and fill it up with his presence. She could smell the slightest hint of cigar smoke, like a raspy note in a singer's voice, she could feel the warmth of his body, see the darkness of his lashes and the burning intensity of his gaze.

"Good," he said, his voice all low and sexy. This was like something out of a fantasy. One of her own fantasies, in fact, from when she was a kid.

But she wasn't a kid anymore. She was all grown up.

She felt as though he leaned toward her but he was so close there wasn't far to lean. She felt as though she leaned toward him, one of those slow motion leans that he probably wrote in his scripts.

A chorus of female laughter, quickly snuffed, reminded her that there was a party winding down, a party to celebrate her engagement. And the man standing so close to her they were practically sharing a bra, the man who made her lips tingle with longing to kiss him, was not the guy she'd agreed to marry.

She pulled away, breaking the spell. "I have to go," she gasped, and then she fled.

BEN WATCHED Ashley disappear into the night, half frustrated and half relieved. What the hell was he thinking? Messing with an engaged woman? Even if it was clear to him that neither bride nor groom were in love with the other, who was he to push his way between them.

He shook his head at his own stupidity. Turned to head back into his pool house where a much-needed cold shower would take the place of the midnight swim he'd come so tantalizingly close to enjoying. He nearly tripped over an object in his path, bent to retrieve it and chuckled softly. "I don't believe it," he said, as he held Ashley's dropped shoe in his hand. "I do not believe it."

He headed back into the pool house and set the shoe on his bedside table. He slept well. In the morning, he carried the shoe out to his work area, put coffee on and waited for the usual splashing outside that indicated his resident mermaid had come for her morning dip. However, no splashing occurred.

She didn't come every single day, but she showed up often enough that not to see her was remarkable. He worked for a bit, but the high-heeled silver sandal sitting in the middle of his glass table was distracting. Every time he saw it he was reminded of that very ill-advised moment last night, standing around the swimming pool, when he'd very nearly made a move on a woman who was not only engaged but living on the same property. And to think that Ashley was the one who had pulled away.

He had a few smart cracks planned to say when she showed up for her swim, foolish comments that would hopefully put the relationship back to the easy familiarity they'd enjoyed before last night. But he never got a chance to use his lines. Work wasn't going very well anyway so finally around eleven he picked up the shoe and decided to deliver it to its rightful owner. He walked down the winding path that would lead him to her cottage. A full team of gardeners and cleaners was busy at work up near the big house removing all traces of yesterday's entertainment. He imagined there were a few sore heads this morning, one of which no doubt belonged to the groom-to-be.

When he reached the cottage he nearly bumped into Ashley coming out the door. She looked much more like the Ashley he knew this morning, wearing a tight jean skirt, sleeveless white shirt and sandals. She carried a big straw bag over one shoulder. When she caught sight of him a slight blush rose on her cheeks. She wasn't a girl who blushed easily, and had he not been looking at her so intently he never would have noticed.

She dragged on her usual cocky attitude to cover any momentary embarrassment as her gaze dropped to the shoe he was holding out to her the way the waiters last night held up trays of champagne. "I wondered where I dropped that," she said, reaching for the shoe.

"Not so fast." He pulled the shoe back before she could touch it. "How do I know it's yours?"

She tilted her head and gave him a quizzical, exasperated look. "You brought that shoe to my house because you saw me wearing it last night. Whose shoe do you think it is?"

He could sense the quiver of amusement and knew that she was trying hard to hold onto her snarky expression. "I should probably make you try on this shoe and then, if it fits, we'll know it's yours."

She seemed to consider the idea. "But then you'll have to kneel at my feet, and you'll get your pretty white pants all dirty."

He gazed at the shoe and then back at her. "That would be a problem. What do we do?"

"I don't know, but we better do it fast." She glanced her watch, a big round timepiece that looked huge on her wrist. It was kind of quirky of her to use an actual watch instead of her cell phone to tell time. "I can't miss my bus or I'll be late for work."

"Bus? There must be half a dozen cars in that massive garage over there."

"At least have a dozen. But, first, none of them are mine, and second, I don't know how to drive." She sounded a little defensive.

"You don't know how to drive?"

"No." She reached for the shoe, "and I really have to go."

"I'll drive you."

"You don't even know where I'm going."

"It doesn't matter. My time is my own."

She glanced at him with sympathy. "The script's not going well at all, is it?"

He pretended to think about it. "I don't know. This morning when I woke up I wrote two lines of dialogue. But after I got my second cup of coffee, I deleted one of them." He shook his head. "No. It's not going well. Maybe a drive will clear my head."

"I work at La Scala, which is a coffee shop with pretensions."

"I don't know where that is, but I'll come with. In fact, maybe I'll bring my laptop and work there." He really liked this idea. He used to write in coffee shops all the time back before he could afford a proper writing studio in his house. Maybe that was what he needed to kick start the script. Maybe he needed noise and people around and chatter and the steam-engine wheeze of an industrial espresso machine. Plus, he was curious about why someone of twenty-five didn't know how to drive.

She withdrew big, dark sunglasses from her bag and prepared to put them on. She glanced at him. "You're not going to be all pervy and weird and keep staring at me while I'm working are you?"

He winced. "I was hoping my charming returning of the shoe would kind of let me off having to apologize."

Her eyes widened in surprise and he saw that faint, faint trace of pink appear once more. "You were going to apologize?"

"No, I wasn't. But now I think I should. I probably drank more than I meant to last night, but I shouldn't have been hitting on you." He was about to add words like it won't happen again, but he stopped himself. He tried never to make promises he couldn't keep. "I'm sorry." He glanced down at her and held out his hand. "Friends?"

The expression in her eyes was hard to read. Most of all he thought he saw confusion. But she nodded and held out her hand. "Friends."

They shook hands solemnly and he felt the warmth of her hand in his plus the strength in her shake. He may tease her about her likeness to Cinderella, but there was nothing helpless about this gun toting, athletic woman. She was strong. He wondered if she knew that.

After she tossed the shoe back in the cottage, she shut the

door once more and they headed together up the path. Even though there was a huge garage for the main house, the pool house had its own parking spot. In it was parked his Ferarri. He didn't go in a lot for the big fancy toys Hollywood was so famous for. Besides, his success was modest by Hollywood standards, though he'd already made more money than he ever dreamed he would from the stories he made out of his head. However, one overpriced ego-boosting toy he had indulged in. That was his car. It was a Ferrari California and he loved that baby. He loved the low-slung body, handling around corners on the coast road, the sun on his face and the wind through his hair when he took the top down.

"Hop in," he said when they reached the car. "I'll run in and grab my laptop."

"You're serious?"

"Serious as unemployment." Which was what he'd face if he didn't get this project completed.

Since he figured his ride was going to be speedier than the bus at getting Ashley to work, he took the time to make sure he packed a paper notebook and his favorite pens as well as his laptop. He ran back out and got in the car. The engine started with a purr of power and he backed out and headed toward the road.

He pushed the remote to open the gates and they motored out onto the private drive.

"Top down?"

She grinned at him. "Oh, yeah."

The sun shone and the sea sparkled. He glanced over to find a huge smile of pure bliss on Ashley's face. In that moment, even through two pairs of dark glasses, their gazes connected and he thought without the double polarized lenses between them their eyeballs might have scorched.

He silently cursed, and dragged his attention back to the road.

CHAPTER 10

*L*a Scala was, as she'd warned him, a lot fancier in name than in reality. He liked that. She walked in ahead of him and he followed more slowly. She raised a hand in greeting to the three baristas currently behind the counter and then disappeared through a side door.

He glanced around the coffee shop. It was like a million other coffee shops and yet had its own personality. There were posters on the wall for various Italian operas, and some decorator had drawn fake pillars and opera scenes on the walls, but other than that, the tables and chairs were pretty standard coffee-shop fare. There were half a dozen faux-leather club chairs, all of them filled. The tables were sparsely populated with people reading newspapers, studying, chitchatting, or, like him, working alone on laptops.

He chose the closest empty table he could find which put him basically dead center in the middle of the coffee shop. It would be the least quiet spot in the place, but then, if he'd wanted quiet, he could have stayed in the pool house.

Having chosen his table, he unpacked his bag, set his notebook and one of his favorite pens out, and then set up his laptop. He removed his jacket and hung it over the chair back and then approached the counter. By this time, Ashley was out front, a dark green apron with the words *La Scala* written in script across the chest. "What can I get you?" she asked.

"I will have a Grande café latte, please."

She flashed him a quick smile. "I love it when my first customer of the day has an easy order." She grabbed a big white pottery mug and began doing whatever it was that baristas did. He moved to the other side of the machine, watching her swift efficiency with a machine so complicated it looked as though it could launch a space mission. When she handed him his drink he noticed the latte art in the foam. "Is that a lightning bolt?"

"Yeah. It is."

"Huh, I usually get a heart."

She rolled her gaze, "so obvious."

When he tried to pay, she waved him away. "One of my only perks is that I can give out free coffees to my friends."

"Thanks," he said. When she turned to serve the next customer he discreetly stuffed a ten-dollar bill into the tip jar.

He took his lightning bolt coffee back to his table and settled down. He opened his computer and pulled up the file for his current script. He sipped his coffee while he went over the last scene. It didn't spring to life. The problem was the woman. "It's always a woman," he muttered to himself, not even realizing he'd spoken aloud until an old man at the table beside him glanced up from his crossword. "You said it."

While he pretended to work, he sipped his coffee and glanced around. Even though he'd promised not to stare at Ashley while she was working, he couldn't keep his gaze from going towards her from time to time. He knew there were thousands of young women like her in the city working at coffee shops. They were budding actresses, budding writers, students, or people who didn't know what else they wanted to do with their lives. Maybe this wasn't her dream job, but she was good.

She moved with graceful efficiency, and when the lunch rush started, and there were four of them back there it was like a choreographed dance the way they stepped and dipped and *do-si-do*'d to avoid each other.

He didn't fully understand why she worked at a coffee shop when there were a thousand opportunities for a young, clearly creative person like her. He also didn't understand why she had no driver's license. In fact, there was a lot about Ashley Carnarvon that he didn't understand, and he found he very much wanted to know all about her. An idea began to form.

He turned back to his screenplay and deleted the entire scene that he had spent the past few days writing, rewriting, and re-re-writing. It wasn't the writing that was the problem. It was the damn woman.

He thought about Ashley and her mother and why women make certain choices, and he started again. He'd been picturing Vanessa Moore in the role of the wife, an older version of Vanessa, but her all the same. No wonder the writing was crap. He imagined Ashley, instead. An older Ashley, but a woman who could easily have married the wrong guy. What would happen if she fell in love with someone else when she was already committed to the wrong man?

He felt an urgency, deep in his gut, that told him he was on the right track. He wrote the scenes straight through, while the fire of inspiration burned. And when he got to the end of the scene he didn't even bother to reread what he'd written.

He knew what he had to do. He had to go back to the very beginning. He wasn't even in the coffee shop anymore. La Scala became a dirty brick alleyway. He could smell stale urine and rank garbage. If he looked into corners he'd find needles. A lone cop entered the alley, humming with tension, ready for a confrontation. A shadowy figure melted out of the shadows of Ben's imagination and his fingers flew.

He jumped when a voice said, "Hey!" From the loudness and

general irritation in the tone, he suspected she'd said it a time or two already. He glanced up to find Ashley staring down at him the way a mother might study a child she suspects has a fever.

"I brought you something to eat. But the way you're going, I figured I better tell you or you wouldn't notice."

He blinked, blinked again and then rubbed his eyes. He'd get eyestrain if he wasn't careful. On the table in front of his laptop was a sandwich, another latte and a glass of water. He looked up at her, only now realizing he was hungry and parched with thirst. "Thank you."

She shook her head, her quirky smile playing over her lips. "You're not the only crazy writer we get in here you know. If you get low blood sugar and pass out it disturbs the other customers."

"What kind of sandwich is this?" He said pulling the plate towards him.

"Do you care?"

He realized, as she must already have done, that he was starving. "No, not really."

"Didn't think so. I gave you today's special."

"When do you get a break? Can you join me?"

"I'm not taking a break today. I need to get to class, and if I skip a break that gives me fifteen extra minutes."

A frown pulled his brows together. "That sounds barbaric. And probably against labor laws. What time do you finish?"

"I get off at three. Why?"

He matched her pissy tone. "Because, if I know what time you get off, I can decide if I want to stay here until then and I could give you a ride to school."

"Why would you drive me around all day?"

He gestured to the food on his plate. "Why would you bring me a sandwich?"

She knew he had him. "Okay, you can drive me to school."

"Good. Now, that buys you fifteen minutes for a break and time to eat something."

He thought she might argue with him or refuse, but again she nodded and walked back behind the counter. A minute later she reappeared through the door she'd passed through when she started her shift, minus her apron, and carrying an identical sandwich to his. Plus her own glass of water.

She sat down across from him, and he immediately shut the lid on his laptop so he had a clear view of her.

"It looks like the work's going well."

He felt tired, creatively drained, and yet still filled with ideas. It was an incredible feeling. "I can't even tell you how amazing this is. I was stuck. Banging my head against a brick wall without realizing that the reason there was a brick wall in front of me is because I'd gone off the path, and left the road."

She swallowed her first bite of sandwich. Sipped water. "So, you're back on the road?"

"It's like I was lost in some dark twisting path and emerged onto a freeway and a Porsche Carrera was sitting there with the engine running and the driver's door open and I jumped in, put the pedal to the floor and started flying. That's how it feels."

"So it's going well then," she said, teasing him now.

He chomped into his sandwich, nodding enthusiastically. "It's going great," he mumbled around his food.

They were both obviously hungry so they ate in silence for a few moments. Then he asked the question that had been bothering him since this morning. "Why don't you know how to drive?"

She sucked a dab of mayonnaise off the end of her finger. He knew she didn't mean it to be a sexy or provocative gesture, but his lizard brain didn't know that and responded.

"Honestly, I don't really know. I wanted to learn how to drive, but when I was a teenager my mother was always busy working or out doing something. And I was busy too. Obviously, she couldn't afford to send me to driver training school, and she didn't have time to teach me. After a while I gave up... I'm not very good at sticking with things."

In fact, he was beginning to believe that it wasn't so much she who gave up as other people who let her down. "Would you still like to learn?"

She placed the last of her sandwich crusts on the plate. For some reason, he found it endearing she didn't eat her crusts. Especially as an identical collection of crusts decorated his own plate. "Learn to drive?"

"Yeah."

She took a sip of water and a moment to think over what he'd asked her. "Yes, yes I would. It's inconvenient as hell taking the bus everywhere. Plus, if I end up having kids, it would sure be easier if I had a driver's license." She took another sip of water. "And a car."

"I'm sure the Van Hoffendams will make certain you get a car."

She shrugged in answer.

"I'll teach you."

She was so shocked at his word that she choked on her drink. She coughed and spluttered and drank down more water. "*You* will teach me to drive?"

He was also shocked by his words, but he liked the idea of teaching Ashley Carnarvon how to drive. "Yes, I will. In case you're wondering, I am an excellent driver."

"I know you're a good driver. You drove me here today."

"I can also tell you that I have never had a speeding ticket," though he had talked himself out of a couple, "and I've never had an accident."

She wrinkled her nose and her diamond stud winked. "What car would I learn on?"

"My car."

She leaned forward, resting her forearms on the table, "Your car? Not that fancy convertible you drove me here in. Isn't it a Lamborghini or something?"

"Ferrari. It's the only car I own."

"But... But, that car must be worth a fortune."

"So what? If you think you'll become a better driver learning on some crappy ancient beater, I can assure you that you won't."

"No, of course not. But if I have an accident in some crappy ancient beater I won't feel as guilty."

"Okay, here's your first driving lesson. And we're going to have it right here at the table in the coffee shop." He put on what he hoped was a very professorial expression. "Never ever imagine that you're going to have an accident. Put the whole idea out of your head. If you are going to think about yourself driving, you will picture yourself in complete control of your vehicle, a fine road warrior."

She glanced at her watch and rose, collecting their dishes from the table. "I need to get back to work. You'll be back at three?"

"Yes. And I'll tell you right now: one of the best things about learning to drive is that you won't have to rely on other people to show up on time. You will be independent."

"If I can ever afford a car."

"Well, a driver's license gets you one step closer to having a car. So, will you let me teach you?"

The dishes and glassware rattled slightly as she shrugged. "I'll think about it."

In fact, he didn't need to return to the coffee shop by three o'clock. He never left. The final two hours of her shift could have been five minutes for all he knew. He was in the zone— that magical place where writing was effortless and ideas tumbled around his head like bingo balls and all he had to do was reach in and grasp them. Because he didn't want to be a complete table hog and cost this fine establishment money, he ordered another coffee that he didn't really want, and bought six brownies out of the display case.

When she came to rouse him at three o'clock he was ridiculously pleased with himself. "I have to thank you," he said, "I had a fantastic day working here." He glanced around. "I don't know what it is, but there's great creative energy in here."

CHAPTER 11

*T*hey left the coffee shop together and got into the gorgeous convertible once more. Ashley had enjoyed watching Ben today as he'd worked. It was funny, but she could tell the moment he got lost in the story. It was as though he went somewhere else. He probably had no idea how cute he looked when he was in the middle of writing.

He was a fast typist, and she could tell when he was really in the zone because his fingers flew across the keyboard. He also interacted with his laptop, so if she hadn't known he was a sought-after screenwriter, she could be forgiven for thinking he was a little crazy. He nodded once in a while, which looked, from the outside, as though he were agreeing with something the laptop had said to him. Sometimes his lips moved. She suspected he was trying out lines of dialogue. A lot of the writers who came in here plugged in to music while they worked, but he didn't do that. Anyway, her shift had certainly passed more quickly with Ben around.

She'd felt nervous this morning when he showed up at her place with her shoe from the night before. She knew that both of them were remembering that strange moment of the almost-kiss.

She could beat herself up all day for letting herself be attracted to the guest in the pool house, but what was the point? She'd been drawn to him since she was fifteen years old. A decade had not made him less interesting or less gorgeous. In fact, the decade had brought him success as a writer, screen credits, a certain polish and sophistication, and, of course, he'd filled out. His face had a few interesting lines, his eyes showed more experience, and when he looked at her she got the feeling that he knew all about pleasing women.

The thought sent a shiver across her skin, so she had to ask him to repeat whatever he'd just said.

"I asked you what time you have to be at school."

"What is it with you and my schedule?"

"I took a few minutes to go online using your coffee shop's excellent free Wi-Fi and discovered that the DMV is open until five o'clock tonight. I thought we might drive over there so you can get your learner's permit."

She stared at him. "You really don't let grass grow, do you."

"Look, I want to make a deal with you. I will teach you to drive. In return, I would really appreciate it if you would read over the scenes that involve the cop's wife in my script."

It was a novel experience for her to be listened to at all, never mind have her opinion solicited by a successful young screenwriter. "Wow. That's some deal. You really want me to read your script?"

"I do. As you made me realize so painfully, I don't understand women as well as I like to think I do. Plus, I kept casting Vanessa Moore in the role, which isn't good as I seriously looked forward to killing off her character."

"You need to cast someone else."

He sent her a glance that was hard to interpret. "Already have. Will you take the deal?"

Oh, what the hell? It was a pain not knowing how to drive and here was a golden opportunity for her to learn. She nodded. "You have a deal."

ASHLEY WASN'T PREPARED when Ben handed her the keys to his car the next morning. She'd come for her usual morning swim, and when she finished, he came out of the pool house with two mugs of coffee. Heaven. She belted her robe over her wet suit and they sat together and drank their coffee.

She put her hand out instinctively when he passed something to her, and only after the bundle of keys hit her palm did she realize what he was doing. She glanced up at him, startled. "Today?"

"Right now, if you like. Come on, don't be chicken. You want to learn to drive, and I want to teach you. There is no time like the present."

She stared down at the keys, winking at her as though daring her to take a chance. "I'm scared."

"If you're more scared of driving than of shooting live weapons, you're crazy."

A sudden grin lit her face. "Okay. But I have to shower and change first."

"I'll wait."

She ran back to the cottage and told herself that millions of people knew how to drive. She'd be fine. But she was nervous when she got behind the wheel of the expensive convertible. She wondered how this adventure was going to turn out as she took her time adjusting the seat and mirrors as her learner's booklet had instructed.

Ben sat beside her, calm and unflappable. "Whenever you're ready," he said.

She imagined herself preparing to shoot something. She

took a deep steadying breath, started the engine, and carefully reversed. Luckily, there were lots of secluded roads in the area. After an hour or so her confidence grew. She could drive in a straight line. She could brake. She could turn right. She could turn left. She could back up. She even attempted parallel parking. Ben offered a little advice, a few tips, and mostly quiet support. When she pulled back in to his parking space in front of the pool house she felt filled with pride at her accomplishment.

"Thank you," she said and leaned across the seat and threw her arms around Ben in an enthusiastic and completely spontaneous hug. She felt the full impact of his body as he hugged her back. How strong he was, how muscular the arms that wrapped around her for just a second too long. Then she pulled back, laughing. "That was so incredible."

"I knew you could do it. You're a good driver. I had a feeling you would be."

"How did you know?"

"Anyone who can walk into what they think is a dangerous situation involving a psycho and a gun and act as cool as you did is not going have any trouble driving—even in LA."

She passed him the keys and got out, still laughing. Only then did she notice Eric. He was sitting on a rock wall that gave him a view of the pool house, and he was watching her.

"Eric! What are you doing here?" She felt an odd anxiety in her belly, as though she'd been caught doing something wrong, when she knew she hadn't.

"I came over here to see if you wanted to hang out. Your mom told me you were out driving with Ben here." He rose slowly from the wall and ambled toward them.

"Ben is teaching me how to drive." She hated the sound of her own voice, all chirpy and fake.

He slid a slow glance between the two of them. "I can teach you to drive." There was an undertone of menace in his voice and she felt Ben bristle as he took a couple of steps toward Eric. This was ridiculous. She wasn't going to have a couple of grown men fight over her. Not that the idea didn't hold a certain appeal. She'd never been fought over before.

However, she preferred to fight her own battles. She walked right up to Eric putting her back to Ben. "Then why didn't you? You've known that I wanted to learn how to drive since I was sixteen years old. You have your own car. You never once offered to teach me."

He gazed down at her. "And you never asked."

It was true, she hadn't. "Well, my lesson is over for today. Do you still want to do something?"

Eric seemed like he was thinking about making a big deal out of this and then she could almost see the moment he decided it was too much effort. He shrugged. "Sure, I guess."

She heard the electronic click behind her as Ben locked the car. The next thing she heard was the pool house door opening and then shutting behind him.

"So, what do you want to do?"

He shrugged. "I don't know. Go to the beach maybe? We could take a Frisbee down, raid your mom's fridge for beer."

He always did this. He showed up at her place, or called her to come over to his with some vague plan that usually involved mooching food or drink off one of their parents. She'd never minded it before, but now that she was contemplating spending her entire life with this guy, she was starting to look at him with a more critical eye.

"Shouldn't you be studying for your stockbroker's exams or something?"

He leaned closer, "would you quit busting my balls all the time?"

"Sorry. You said when we got engaged that you'd find a job."

"And I will." He kicked a pebble with his foot. "My Dad's been talking to me about joining his company."

"Wow. Will you join your dad's firm?" He'd always said he'd rather dig ditches.

"I don't know. Maybe." He kicked another pebble. "Sometimes it all seems kind of intense, you know? Getting married, getting a real job with a suit and tie and stuff? The whole thing's kind of stressing me out."

She understood how he felt. Normally she never would've nagged him about getting a job. But now she saw herself falling into the role of wife. The more she thought about it the more she wondered how well they really knew each other. She took a breath and said, "We did kind of rush into this. I mean the engagement and everything. It's all happened so fast. But it's our life. We can take some more time if you want."

His gaze flew up to meet hers and she thought she saw panic cross his face. "No." Then he moved closer, giving her the charming look that always made her toes curl. "Unless you've changed your mind about me?" He kissed her softly before she had a chance to speak. And he bumped his body up flush against hers, kissing her more deeply. Then he grabbed her hand and pulled her, laughing, toward the beach.

She was lounging on the sand with Eric when her cell phone rang. They were sharing a beer, though she'd made him go to the store and buy his own rather than raid her mother's fridge. She checked her call display and saw a local number, one she didn't recognize. "Hello?"

"Hi Ashley, this is Tasmine. We met at your engagement party the other night."

She knew exactly who Tasmine was; what she didn't know was how she'd got hold of her number. She certainly hadn't given it to her mother-in-law's choice of bridesmaid. "Hi, Tasmine," she let the surprise sound in her voice, and while holding the phone to her ear, glanced at Eric with her eyebrows raised. His mother didn't have her cell phone number either.

The only way Tasmine could have got her number was from Eric.

He sent her his most innocent look, the one he usually wore when he pulled one of his pranks, and she shook her head at him.

"I hope you don't mind me calling you of the blue like this, but I was wondering if we could get together and talk about the wedding."

"Wow, you're keen."

The other woman laughed. "I've been involved in enough weddings to know how important it is to nail down the basics as soon as possible. I am really good with details, I thought I might bring a binder with me of a wedding that was similar to yours, and you could see if there's anything you like."

"You have binders?"

A burst of laughter met her question, "I did warn you, I am very organized."

"Well, now's a good time. Would you like to come over here?"

Eric started shaking his head violently and waving his hands: No, no, no! She ignored him.

If Eric was going to give her number to pushy bridesmaids, he could remain by her side while said pushing bridesmaid arrived at her house with binders.

"Absolutely. Now would be great."

She gave the woman directions and told her that she'd meet her at the cottage.

She ended the call and glared at Eric. "You gave my phone number to Tasmine and didn't bother to tell me?"

He played dumb. "My mom asked me for your number. I didn't know what it was for."

"And you didn't ask why she wanted it?" Or was he really that dumb?

"Figured it was for wedding stuff."

"Well, your mother pushed this bridesmaid on me. She's

some kind of distant cousin of yours and she said you used to play together as kids."

"It's a pretty big family. I don't remember every kid I played with in the sandbox."

"Well, Tasmine remembered you. I think she had a crush on you when you were kids."

"Happens to all the girls," he teased. A shadow fell across her face as he leaned over her. "But you're the one I chose," he said, all low and sexy.

She kissed him and then pulled away. "Come on, I have to clean up the cottage before she gets here."

"So you're kicking me out so you can huddle with your bridesmaids?"

She set her voice to steel. "Do not even think about leaving me alone with that woman."

He must have realized that she was serious. Reluctantly he followed her up to the cottage where she rapidly tidied up the small living room and made sure the kitchen table was clean and free of any breakfast crumbs.

Tasmine arrived with a briefcase. She wore white linen pants and a mint green silk tank under a sweater jacket. She looked like the CEO of her own empire, with a dash of cheerleader thrown in. Ashley looked like the CEO of Club Loser in her short cutoffs and bare feet. She was pretty sure there was sand stuck to her back.

"You're working? On a Saturday?"

"I'm a sales rep for a design company. I set my own hours, but I often end up working Saturdays." She shrugged, "Life in the fast lane, right?"

She stepped inside and faltered. "Oh, hi Eric. I didn't realize you'd be here."

"Little woman insisted," he grumbled. "Not even married yet, I'm already whipped."

She let out a trill of delicious laughter. "Oh, don't be silly. Of course you're not. Ashley wants to make sure you're involved in every step of the wedding. The most successful weddings are the ones where the groom takes an active role."

Eric did not look thrilled with the idea of being an active participant in his own wedding. He had his feet up on the couch and was busily interacting with his cell phone.

Ashley said, "Why don't we go to the kitchen, so we have more room to spread out?"

With a last glance at Eric, Tasmine said, "Sure." She followed Ashley into the kitchen and settled herself at the table. "This is such a darling cottage. How lucky are you to live right by the beach?"

"I know. Would you like some tea? Coffee? A glass of wine?"

"I'd love a glass of water if you have one."

She poured Tasmine a glass of water and a second one for herself, then settled at the table. Tasmine reached into her briefcase and pulled out a binder, which she set in front of Ashley. She also pulled out a tablet computer and began scrolling.

"That was such a fun engagement party the other night," Tasmine said. Then she leaned closer, like they were best friends enjoying a secret. "I didn't know that Bennett Saegar was living here. Oh, what that poor man has been through. That actress should be shot. And the way the media has blown it all out of proportion? Makes me sick. It's so nice of your family to give him a place to stay."

Ashley hadn't realized Bennett Saegar was that famous. She asked, "Did he tell you all this?"

"As if. No, I read it online. I keep up with the news, especially Hollywood news. It's part of my business to know what's going on."

Ashley opened the binder and looked over a few pages. There were tabs for gift registry, florist, photographer, guest list, and so on. Maybe she wasn't the sharpest knife in the drawer, but Ashley prided herself on being smarter than a butter knife. She glanced up at Tasmine and tried to look tough and steely even with sand skittering down her spine.

"You are a professional, aren't you? I'm guessing Grace hired you and she's planting you in the bridal party as a spy." It was more than she'd meant to say, but not more than she'd been thinking ever since this overenthusiastic bridesmaid was first shoved at her.

Tasmine didn't look particularly surprised to be busted. She put her elbows on the table and for a moment Ash was sorry that she'd so carefully scrubbed off the spilled raspberry jam that had congealed in exactly the spot where Tasmine placed her right elbow. "Honestly, I suggested to Grace that she tell you up front. I'm not big on subterfuge."

"That's a big word for lying."

Tasmine shook her head. "None of it was a lie, technically. I am a cousin, though a distant one, and one summer my family did come up and hang out. I played with Eric, as I said I did. And I have been a bridesmaid in almost a dozen weddings. All that is true. However, you're right. I've made a side business out of it. I'm a professional bridesmaid with a sideline in wedding planning."

"I've picked my own bridesmaids thanks."

"Look, think about it for a moment. There's a reason brides hire me."

"Or their future mothers-in-law hire you," she muttered.

"Or that." She set the tablet down and gave Ashley her full focus. "I met your bridesmaids the other night. Really great gals and I can see why you chose them. But they're also super busy and didn't seem like they had really embraced the bridesmaid role as enthusiastically as I would like to see. I can pick up the slack." She glanced significantly toward the doorway that led to where Eric was lounging. "Or between you and your future mother-in-law. I will do ten times the work of a normal brides-maid. I am truly organized, I've got fabulous contacts, and I can make your journey a lot easier. Getting married is stressful; there's a lot more planning than you realize. I can help with that."

She hated feeling manipulated, even though everything Tasmine said made sense. "I don't know."

"Here's what I propose. I'll leave that binder with you. Look it over." Her fingers flew over her tablet for a few moments and then Ashley heard a text message alert on her smart phone. "I just texted you a list of references. These are brides who've hired me. Talk to them, then let me know what you want to do."

"But I didn't hire you. It's Grace who should get your references."

For the first time Tasmine looked slightly less perky than usual. She leaned in slightly. "I get a lot of requests. I'm not desperate for business, believe me. I told Grace I'd do this, but I'm not interested in helping someone who does not want my help."

"You're saying I can fire you?"

"Absolutely." She gathered her things and rose.

When she got to the door she turned. "Oh, and one last thing?"

"Yes?"

"I'm very photogenic. I look great in wedding photos." Then she winked and was gone.

"What was that about?" Eric asked as she closed the door behind Tasmine.

She turned to him, "Tasmine hires herself out as a bridesmaid."

Eric's face wrinkled in puzzlement. "What do you mean she hires herself?"

"I mean, she gets paid to be a bridesmaid. And your mother hired her."

She might've suspected that Eric knew all about his mother's plot to plant a hired bridesmaid in her bridal party except that no one could fake shock that well. "Girls want to be bridesmaids so badly they do it as a job?"

He put down his phone and sat up. "Hey, maybe that's what I should do. I should rent myself out as a classy groomsman. What do you think?"

"I think that in order to get paid you would have to do a lot more work than simply showing up and looking cute."

"Damn. I knew it was too good to be true." He picked up his phone again and settled back on the couch.

She watched him for a minute. They hadn't talked anymore about her getting driving lessons from Ben so she settled on the end of the couch, pushing his feet out of the way so she could sit down. "You seemed kind of upset that Ben gave me a driving lesson."

"I was surprised. That's all."

"I do want to learn how to drive. It's a pain not having a license."

"Yeah. I get it."

"But, if *you* want to teach me how to drive, that would be cool."

She could almost hear his thought process, she'd known him so long. In the end, as she had suspected, his laziness won out over his jealousy. "No, that's okay. If you say he's just a friend, then I believe you."

"And you're okay with it if he teaches me to drive?"

He shrugged. "You're right. It's lame that you don't even know how to drive. I don't want to have to drive everywhere when we're married. This way you can be my designated driver when I get wasted."

"Such an incentive to get my license."

CHAPTER 12

*E*ric took her out for sushi, and then, since he was playing poker with the boys, dropped her off back home.

The cottage was dark and quiet exactly the way she liked it. Her mom had met a man online and was on her second date. When she was between boyfriends, she tended to grill Ashley about the details of her life as though trying to live vicariously through her. She had the kind of mom who would share clothes with her, except that Melody was a smaller size, a fact she knew thrilled her mother to her pedicured toenails.

Whatever.

When she was dating, she tended to give her daughter more space. Ashley shut the door to her room and booted up her laptop. She knew she should pay more attention to the news but it was so violent and depressing most of the time that she didn't bother. Her uncle talked politics endlessly so she knew how a staunch republican of a certain age might view the world, and she knew there were things going on out there that deserved her outrage, but she found it easier not to know.

However, Tasmine's little speech about Ben had her curious.

He'd told her briefly why he was here but she hadn't realized that even someone like Tasmine might know the details.

She typed in a Google search of Bennett Saegar plus *Ravensong* and was shocked at how fast the hits appeared.

And she had to admit after reading for half an hour that if she didn't know Ben, she'd think he was a manipulative user who would take an innocent woman's trust, her talent and her love, and then suck her dry. Although she was cynical enough to wonder why a woman recovering from near death by suicide had so much energy for giving interviews.

Also, from the photos of her in her hospital bed, it was obvious she'd used makeup to make herself even more waiflike. Her huge blue eyes were outlined in black and everything else, including her lipstick, was white. She even wore white, filmy nightgowns as she gave interviews from the private convalescent home.

Ben had outdone himself. He'd got involved with a woman who was both a bimbo and a victim, but also cunning enough to use both to her advantage.

She was reading through a particularly juicy blog called *LA Insider*. Dotted throughout were photos of the filming of *Ravensong*, and one, which all the online news magazines had also published, showed Ben and Vanessa Moore in close conversation.

She was shaking her head, about to turn off her computer for the night, when a new headline caught her attention.

Diva Designer Cursed

She'd have scrolled past, except she saw a photograph of a wedding gown that looked a lot like—Oh, no, Oh, crap... it was the same gown she'd be wearing when she married Eric. There were no others like it in the world. It was a one-off design.

What?

She read on:

Evangeline and a wedding gown she designed are cursed, according to inside sources from the design house of Evangeline.

It's an open secret that the former model and actress turned wedding gown designer only designs for the rich and beautiful. What's not so well known is that the famous Brit is a shrew when it comes to treating her staff. "She's so demanding, she throws fits if everything's not absolutely perfect," said a source, who asked not to be named. The source, who works closely with the Diva Designer, said that during a final fitting of the wedding gown she designed for Kate Winton-Jones's marriage to uber-eligible bachelor Edward Carnarvon, the designer flew into a rage and fired an underling on the spot. The angry woman, said to be of gypsy origin, cursed both the dress and its designer.

"The Romani have very powerful magic," the same source told us.

Within days, the bride disappeared from sight and pretty soon the wedding was cancelled. Coincidence? Maybe. The dress is set to make an appearance at a lesser celebrity wedding, when Eric Van Hoffendam, youngest son of Charles and Grace Van Hoffendam, marries a Carnarvon cousin.

Evangeline's press office said she was unavailable to comment, but strangely, no one's seen the Diva Designer in public since the curse.

Ashley didn't feel sleepy anymore. She slumped to her bed. Cursed? Somebody had cursed her hand-me-down wedding gown? It was bad enough wearing a castoff on the one day that was supposed to be all about her, but did they have to hand down a curse?

Could curses even be handed down?

She went back to her search engine and typed in, 'Can a curse be handed down?' then scoffed at herself. She was twenty-five, not twelve. That article had about as much credibility as the one about Ben causing a suicide.

And this Carnarvon cousin needed to go to bed.

She slammed the lid shut on her computer and dragged on her pajamas. While she brushed her teeth, she decided that being stuck here with her mother and Carnarvon relatives was a much bigger curse.

Still, she took her phone into bed with her and texted Eric.

"Wish you were here."

"Me too." He then proceeded to tell her all the things he wanted to do to her.

She powered down the phone. She'd kind of wanted to hear that he loved her or something, not indulge in a sexting session.

She didn't sleep well. Discovering her wedding dress was cursed kept her awake. And when she did dream, the dress kept intruding, like a creepy stalker, following her around in her dreams. "Stop it!" she finally yelled and the sound of her own agitated voice woke her up.

Not sure if she was becoming unhinged, or whether she was in some kind of Gypsy curse danger, she did what she always did when confronted with a tricky problem. She called Whitney and Sienna and asked them to meet her at Wainrights.

When she arrived, she snagged a table, ordered a craft beer and waited. She didn't mind that they were a few minutes late since she'd had a busy day. A driving lesson in the morning—in which Ben had shown diabolically cruel tendencies in making her parallel park in spaces even a Smartcar would have trouble fitting into—and then she'd spent two hours in a history lecture that was so dull she wondered how people had lived through the actual time period without dying en masse of boredom.

"So, I wanted to talk to you guys," she began when they arrived, wondering how to bring up a curse, and whether a few more drinks should be consumed first.

"Hey, I'm sorry," Sienna said, putting one hand in the air as though bargaining for peace. "I'm totally sorry for being a bad bridesmaid. I know we're supposed to be doing stuff, but honestly, work's so hectic, and Bradley's been acting like a big baby and wants my attention all the time. But I will carve out some time next week, I promise."

"It's okay," she'd chosen bridesmaids for how much she liked them, not for how efficient they'd be, she reminded herself.

"We're organizing your bachelorette party. We're on it, right Sienna?"

"Absolutely," Sienna said, scrunching up her face and staring at the table. No one was a worse liar than Sienna.

"That's not why I wanted to get together," she said, then took a deep breath. "I found an article on the Internet that said my wedding dress is cursed."

Whitney had been checking out the crowd, and now turned. "Sorry, what's that about the curse? You'll have it on your wedding day?"

"Bummer."

"No. Not *the* curse. *A* curse." She stared at the two puzzled faces sitting across from her. "I found an article online about the dress designer, Evangeline. And my dress. It said that Evangeline went postal on some poor seamstress and the woman turned around and cursed both Evangeline and the dress."

"You can't curse Evangeline. She used to live with UK's sexiest man alive, Grant Bakersfield."

"I guess the seamstress didn't know that because she cursed both the designer and the dress. And now I have the dress."

She was glad she'd already confessed that her dress was a hand-me-down so she didn't have to go into it all again. They could concentrate on the curse part.

"Wow."

"So, my question is, can a dress be cursed?"

Whitney snorted and leaned back, which meant she was about to tell a story. "Oh, yeah. My blue Zac Posen? The one I got on sale at Barney's? Totally cursed. Seriously, the first time I wore it this hideous toad kept hitting on me and left sweat marks where he'd had his hand on my shoulder. I am not kidding. I had this big, meaty handprint sweated into my back. So I had the dress cleaned, and then the second time I wore it, Bradley broke up with me."

"Bradley broke up with you?"

She waved a hand. "Only for about thirty minutes. He was having an artistic crisis. But the point is, I'm never wearing that dress again. It's totally cursed."

"So, what do you think? Should I tell my aunt I can't wear the dress she gave me because it's cursed?"

The three of them pondered the problem. Finally, Whitney, the budding lawyer said, "You've got to look at both sides of the argument. If you don't wear the dress, you possibly avoid this alleged curse, but then Millicent will be pissed at you which might be a bigger curse." They all nodded.

"Or, you suck it up and wear the dress, and everybody's happy."

"Assuming the dress isn't actually cursed."

"Right, or that the curse can't be handed down along with the dress."

This whole conversation was making her feel morbid and sorry for herself. "I've had everything else handed down, why not a curse?"

Sienna said, "Look on the bright side."

"Okay," she said, waiting.

Sienna seemed to search her brain. "I can't think of anything, I'm sorry."

The night out with her bridesmaids didn't help her solve the problem of the cursed dress, but it did clarify one thing for her.

Her friends were great but they were busy as hell and not the most reliable pair. She needed Tasmine the hired bridesmaid. As much as it irked her that Grace had hired her a bridesmaid and secret wedding planner, she realized after her two besties left the bar promising to call her the following week that she needed the help.

Tasmine's phone number wasn't very hard to find: it was plastered all over the wedding binder. When she called and officially asked her to sign on as bridesmaid, Tasmine didn't sound very surprised. "Sure, I'd love to," she said, as though she were delighted to organize the wedding of someone she barely knew and then stand up in a dress she'd never wear again to pose for pictures that would fill other people's photo albums. Whatever. Ashley supposed there were worse ways to make money.

Ashley read over the article online about Evangeline and her cursed wedding dress a couple more times. She sent it to Whitney and Sienna to read. She didn't like the uneasy, almost queasy, feeling she experienced when she contemplated wearing that dress down the aisle. She knew there was supposed to be something borrowed that the bride carried down the aisle with her, but she didn't want her borrowed item to be a curse!

CHAPTER 13

There were very few people she could talk to about the curse business. Eric was out of the question. His contribution to the wedding so far had been bringing over a lot of brochures for her to look at for their honeymoon. He seemed a lot more pumped about a tropical vacation than he did about the details of their actual marriage. He talked vaguely about his stockbroker course, but she didn't think he'd registered yet. Nevertheless, Eric was one of those people who always landed on his feet. She imagined he'd work it out.

There was one person who would know all about the curse. Well, there were several who would know the details. The dress designer, Evangeline, obviously, a woman far too terrifying for Ashley to approach. The seamstress who had placed the curse in the first place, but how would she even find such a person? And, finally, the bride for whom the dress was originally designed. Kate Winton-Jones.

Ashley knew her, obviously, because she'd been engaged to her cousin Ted, who used to live in the pool house on this very property. He'd know how to contact her. If anyone knew how bad this curse was and what form it took, that person had to be Kate Winton-Jones.

After thinking about it for a day, she texted Ted. *Hey Ted*, she began. That was easy. How to continue? She didn't want to tell him the truth or he'd scoff at her superstitious nature, so she said: *I need to get hold of Kate. No biggie, just had a question for her. Can you send me her deets?*

She pushed send, then threw her bathing suit on for a morning swim. It wasn't that she intended to see Ben, but she knew there was a good chance that he'd be hard at work in the pool house, that he'd wave when he saw her and go put on a pot of fresh coffee. When she was done, he'd bring her out a mug and they would chat for a few minutes. Maybe he'd offer her another driving lesson. Also, she needed the exercise. She wasn't hung over from the night before with her girlfriends, but she had that slightly fuzzy feeling that one less beer last night would have been a good idea.

Before she dove into the pool, she gazed through the big window and saw the screenwriter in his usual position, bent over his keyboard. He glanced up as though he felt her scrutiny. She waved and he waved back and before she dove in he raised his coffee mug and pointed to it and she gave him the two thumbs up sign. Oh yeah, she would definitely crave a coffee when she finished her swim.

She slipped off her flip-flops, dropped her towel and the big gray T-shirt she wore as a cover-up onto a handy lounger, then dove into the clean, cool water. When she was in the pool, everything seemed solvable. Every part of her worked in rhythm when she was swimming. She always felt like she was getting somewhere even though it was only back and forth across the same stretch of water, like so much of her life. When she finished, she dragged herself out, breathing heavily. As though he'd been watching for her, Ben emerged from the pool house carrying two mugs of coffee. He waited for her to towel off and throw on the oversized T-shirt, then passed her a mug. They settled on a couple of loungers and she sipped gratefully.

"You really had a mission this morning," Ben said, looking at her over the rim of his coffee mug. "The way the water was churning I thought there was a shark attack in the pool."

No wonder she was breathing so hard. She hadn't realized how fast she was swimming. He must've read the expression on her face correctly, for he asked, "is something bothering you?"

And, strangely, for all the people in her life who she felt she couldn't tell about her worries over the cursed—make that possibly-cursed—dress, she felt that Ben was one person who might actually understand. "If I ask you something, will you promise not to think I'm crazy?"

Without hesitation he shook his head. "No way. I retain all rights at this moment and into the future to think of you as crazy."

She couldn't help but grin. "Okay, since you already think I'm crazy, I don't suppose it matters. But here's the problem." She then described to him the article she had read and her fears about the dress being cursed. He listened intently, and didn't laugh, or scoff. "Do you believe in curses?" she asked finally.

He sat quietly for a moment. The endless sun glinted off the pool. "I think that's an interesting question. Do I believe in curses? I don't know. I think curses probably work both ways. What I mean by that is, let's say someone curses me and tells me all my hair will fall out. I have to believe it enough for my hair to fall out. If I don't put credence in the curse, I personally think my hair will stay on my head just fine."

She sipped her coffee. He made good coffee. Her breath was coming back to normal now and she had that blissful sense of relaxation that a good session in the pool always gave her. "So, even if that woman did curse the dress, if I don't believe in curses, you're saying it can't hurt me?"

"Remember, I'm not an exorcist, I'm not a gypsy, I'm merely

a guy who makes up stories for a living. I'm giving you my take on curses. But I could be completely wrong."

"You're probably right." She glanced up at him and felt awareness ripple across her skin the way the breeze rippled the surface of the pool. "My problem is, maybe I do believe a curse may have hit me."

"Yes, that would be a problem. Why do you?"

"I don't know. I feel like everything's going so fast and every-body is so excited about this wedding, and people are throwing us parties and putting ads in the paper and delivering designer dresses. It's too easy. Maybe I'm waiting for the other shoe to drop."

He regarded her seriously for a moment. "I don't think you should do anything because it's easy."

Easy? She wasn't doing that, was she? She did love Eric. It felt good to be doing something right for a change, to feel like this wedding was making two very difficult families happy. Eric didn't seem to have any doubts, why did she?

Of course she didn't share any of this with Ben. What she said was, "I texted Ted and asked him for Kate Winton-Jones's contact information. She's the woman he was supposed to marry. She's the one who was first supposed to wear the dress. If anyone knows about the curse, it will be Kate."

He looked unimpressed by this logic. "You could just get a new dress."

"Oh don't think I haven't thought about it. But to throw this engagement present back in Millicent and Duncan's face? When things are going so well?" She shuddered. "I keep thinking it's just one day, just one dress."

"A pretty important day. And a pretty important dress."

"I'll see what Kate says. Then I'll decide what to do."

"So, how do you feel about a driving lesson today?"

"I have to be at school at two o'clock." She turned to him. "Could our driving lesson take me there?"

He sent her a crooked grin. "And after that, I'm guessing you'd like a second lesson, that would involve driving back from school?"

She twinkled at him. "There's an amazing coffee shop on campus, you'd get so much work done there."

"Tell you what, if our driving lessons get you to and from school, will you come over tonight, and read this new scene I wrote?"

"Deal."

Ashley went home and showered and ate fruit and yogurt for breakfast. She was trying to drop a few pounds for the wedding, though it wasn't going very well. All the swimming and dieting in the world wouldn't make her look like a lily. Her build was athletic, muscular rather than wispy. God, maybe it was the dress that was cursed to have her stuffed in it.

When she'd cleaned up the dishes, she checked her email and found that Kate Winton-Jones had contacted her.

Her email was short and to the point. "Hi Ashley, Ted says you're looking for me. What's up? I'd love to hear from you. Obviously this is my email, and here's my cell number. Call anytime."

She grabbed her cell phone and called the number Kate had provided. Her former almost cousin-in-law answered right away. "Kate Winton-Jones."

"Hey Kate, it Ashley."

"Ashley. It's a good to hear from you." And the weird thing was, she did sound happy to hear from her.

Now that she had Kate on the other end of the phone, she didn't know how to go on. How could she ask a perfectly sensible, intelligent, educated woman whether she thought her wedding dress might be cursed?

She scrambled around for something to say and came up with, "I have some news. I'm getting married."

There was a stunned moment of silence, and then Kate said, "Really? Who are you marrying?"

"Eric Van Hoffendam, of course."

"Eric Van Hoffendam... He's the tall, blond one, right?"

"Yeah, that's the one."

"Well that's wonderful, have you set a date?"

"Four weeks from Saturday."

"Wow. That's so soon."

"I'm not pregnant." She got that out of the way. "We decided to get married and didn't see the point in waiting around for a year or more. We're getting married here on the Carnarvon estate, so we didn't have to book a venue a year in advance."

"Sure, that makes sense."

There was a tiny pause. She wished she had the courage to bring up the curse, but how did you ask someone if they had run off before their own wedding because their stupid dress was cursed? It would make both of them sound nuts.

It was Kate who broke the silence. "This feels sort of weird, but I should probably tell you that I'm getting married too."

"What!"

Kate laughed. "I know, it sounds so crazy. But, being engaged to Ted taught me a lot of things. I was settling. And when I met the man I love, the man I think I'll love forever, well, you know how it is. When it's real love, you know it right deep down. You can't fake real love. You either feel it or you don't."

"Absolutely, I know exactly what you mean." When in fact she wasn't certain that she did. "So, when are you getting married?

"This weekend. On Catalina Island. It's a super small wedding. But why don't you come?"

"No, that's okay. I really hope you'll be happy."

"Ashley, I'm serious. No one named Carnarvon will be there. My mother's not even coming. It's going to be a really small wedding. A few of my close friends, a few of Nick's close friends. I do a lot of things now by instinct when I used to plan everything, and I really feel like you should come."

"I've never been to Catalina Island." Which was weird since it was so close, and if it was a really small wedding and everything was casual, maybe there'd be an easy way to work into the conversation some questions about that dress. "Sure. I'd love to come. Is it okay if I bring a guest?"

"Of course. We're getting married outside, on the beach, it's not like we have to count chairs."

CHAPTER 14

She phoned Eric right away. "Hey babe, what's up?" He asked in his sleepy way.

"Can you come with me to a wedding on Saturday?"

"This Saturday?"

He must be mentally going through his list of the weddings they both had to attend and coming up blank. "I thought we had a weekend off from weddings."

"We do, but this one just came up. It's sort of spontaneous, but it's Kate Winton-Jones, the woman who was supposed to marry my cousin Ted. She invited us to her wedding. I'd love to go."

"I can't, Ash. I've got to go golfing with my dad and some of his buddies."

"You're going golfing with your dad?"

"Yeah." He did not sound very happy. "It's guys he knows who could maybe hire me when I finish my stockbroking course. If I blow it off he'll never shut up about it."

"Okay, I understand. Have fun, and please take a selfie of you in golfing pants, and promise me you'll wear a plaid cap."

"Hey, I can rock a plaid cap." And he was probably right. If anyone could make a tartan hat sexy, it was Eric. He continued, "So, you want to hang out this afternoon?"

"Can't, I have class."

"Okay. Hey, I think I've narrowed it down to Tahiti and Bora Bora."

He was obviously talking about their honeymoon. "Bora Bora? I didn't even know it was on the list."

"It wasn't, but the travel agent found this really cool resort. It's like seven stars or something and there's a million sports, diving and snorkeling and racing boats. It looks awesome. Oh, and there's a spa for you."

"That sounds cool."

"I sent you the link."

"I'll check it out."

She tried not to feel disappointed. Of course Eric had plans on a Saturday. Golfing with his dad? He must really be getting serious about finding a job and getting on with his life. Which was good, she reminded herself. It was very good. Just sort of boring and not Eric.

"I CAN'T FIT into that spot," she argued. "And anyway, it's the wrong side."

"You can do it," Ben replied in his soothing driving instructor tone. "And it's not the wrong side, it's just going in on the left-hand side instead of always parking on the right-hand side of the street."

She huffed out an irritated breath even though she liked the new challenges he kept heaping on her. The truth was, she was an excellent driver, and they both knew it. She reversed the car, which handled like a dream, until the rear wheels were even with the car in front of the spot. She spun the steering wheel, backed into the spot and aced her parallel park.

"Nice job," he said.

"Thanks, I have a good teacher."

"You do. But I have an excellent student."

"Can I go on the highway again?" She loved cruising along the highway with the top down.

"Sure, you've earned it. You know, you could take the test. I think you'd pass."

"Oh." In truth, she hadn't even thought about taking her road test. She loved her driving lessons. She loved driving Ben's car and liked having him sitting beside her either giving her calm advice or driving tips. As she grew more confident, he let her drive and they talked about anything and everything. If she passed the driving test, she'd lose all that. Plus, it wasn't like she had a car to drive. "Can we keep practicing one more week?"

"Absolutely. You should feel completely confident before you take your road test." She might be mistaken, but she thought he sounded relieved that they were continuing their lessons at least for another week.

An idea sprang into her head. "You know what would be really good for my driving?"

"No, but I am guessing your idea will involve huge inconvenience to me and my car."

Damn, he could see right through her. "I was going to invite you to Catalina Island for the day on Saturday. But if you don't want to go, that's fine, I won't take you."

He turned his head to stare at her. "You know they don't allow cars on Catalina Island, right?"

No, she didn't know that, but she wasn't going to let him in on her lack of knowledge. She said, "Of course I know that. But we have to drive down to where you get the ferry." Which she knew was somewhere south of them. She'd look online to find exact directions.

"What's the big attraction with Catalina Island?"

"A wedding."

"A wedding? Who's getting married?"

"Kate Winton-Jones."

He nodded, understanding the entire plan before she even had to say a word. It was great being with someone who was so intuitive. It saved her so much explaining. "Of course. You can ask her about the dress."

"Exactly."

He thought about it for a few minutes. "I guess I can take a day off Saturday, sure."

THE WEDDING of Kate and Nick could not have been more different from the wedding that had been planned for Kate Winton-Jones and Edward Carnarvon III. Ashley wore one of her favorite summer dresses, a blue and black frock designed by a woman in art college in LA. With it she wore chunky black sandals and plenty of sunscreen.

Ben looked both casual and elegant in the same beige chinos that he'd worn to her engagement party, along with a brown linen jacket. He let her drive and they laughed and chatted the entire ride down and then they got the ferry from Dana point. It was easy to pick out the other guests who were on their way to the wedding because they also carried gift-wrapped packages and wore casual finery.

Ashley was a pretty friendly person and soon there was a laughing group of people on their way to the wedding. She met Nick's work associates, and friends of Kate's she had never met before. Kate had only been part of her life because of Ted, so it was strange to find herself going to this wedding, and yet it felt somehow right. Cursed or not, that dress connected them somehow and connected their fates. She didn't understand why, but she was certain of it.

When the ferry docked and they walked down to the boardwalk, there were Kate and Nick standing there, greeting the guests themselves. Instead of the Evangeline-designed down, Kate wore a white cotton sundress, a big straw hat, and sandals. Her groom was equally casual. He wore jeans, a blue and white button-down shirt, and canvas deck shoes. There was no denying the glow of happiness that enveloped the two of them. They held hands as though they couldn't bear not to touch each other. They greeted each guest separately, warmly, and when Ashley reached the bride and groom, Kate gave her an impulsive hug. "I am so glad you came."

In that moment Ashley remembered that the last time they had seen each other, Kate had given her the gel falsies Evangeline had provided to help Kate fill out that dress. Naturally, Ashley didn't need them to fill out the dress, but they were fun to wear.

Before she could introduce her guest, Nick was holding out his hand, "You must be Eric."

"I am not Eric," Ben replied. He held out his hand. "I'm Ben. And this is an awesome wedding."

Ashley said quickly, before anyone could get any ideas, "Eric couldn't make it today. He had a prior commitment. Ben is a friend of mine. He's teaching me to drive."

"Good. It's about time you learned to drive," Kate said. She turned to Ben. "Although Ashley did help me steal a bike one time."

She laughed. "I did, didn't I? Did you keep it?"

Kate shook her head. As if. "I think Ted put it back in the shed and no one ever even noticed it was gone. It wasn't much of a life of crime, but I enjoyed it while it lasted."

She would never forget the sight of the brokenhearted Kate getting on one of the old ten speeds wearing a reflective jacket that was both moldy and miles too big for her over an elegant dress, and pedaling away in high heels as though the hounds of hell were after her.

"That was the night I met Nick."

Of course it was. No wonder they were connected.

They walked, all of the wedding party together, up to the spot where the wedding would take place. It was on a bluff overlooking the ocean. There was no flower-decked arch, no bridesmaids and groomsmen. There was the bride, the groom, her maid of honor, a vibrant looking Latina woman named Lissa, and Nick's best man, who turned out to be his brother. The wedding guests stood around however they liked, or, if they wanted to sit down, there was plenty of room on the grass. The officiant was an older man who wore a blazer over a *Grateful Dead* T-shirt. He kept the ceremony short, but even so, she felt a lump in her throat as these two people who were so clearly in love pledged their love and their lives to each other.

The wedding reception was held at a local restaurant. Everyone was happy. There was an informal vibe, like this was a group of old friends and new friends meeting and enjoying each other's company and the happiness of this beautiful day. After a while, in a gesture that seemed more spontaneous than planned, Nick had the proprietor of the restaurant bring out chilled champagne and waiters carried around trays of the sparkling wine. When everyone had a drink, Nick grabbed Kate's hand and brought her into the center of the restaurant.

Everyone circled around them and a hush fell over the crowd. As Ashley looked across at Nick and Kate, she knew what love felt like. Just watching the two of them stare into each other's eyes she felt that gut-deep resonance. She turned to search out Ben and found him walking towards her, an intent expression in his eyes. He drew up beside her and took her hand. She didn't care at the moment if they were just friends, more than friends, or I-wish-we-could-be more than friends. She linked her fingers with his, enjoying the warm current between them.

Nick cleared his throat, looked at his bride and said, "I will never forget, for as long as I live, the moment I first saw Kate. It was in a restaurant on a busy Friday night. When I saw her, I was first blown away by her beauty, as everyone with eyes can see." Kate rolled her eyes and shook her head but all the same she blushed. Nick grinned at her, and continued, "Then she looked up and caught me staring at her. Normally, when a girl catches you staring, you pretend it was an accident and you look away. But I couldn't. She gazed at me with those big blue eyes and I felt like a bomb went off in my chest. Nobody ever tells you that falling in love's going to hurt, that it's as uncomfortable as a bomb going off in your chest, but trust me, if you've never experienced it? That's what it feels like.

"So I'm sitting there, with this massive detonation going on inside me and I somehow know that my life just changed forever. There are all kinds of songs and poems and I won't embarrass all of us by reciting any of them but they're all about love at first sight. Frankly, I never believed there was any such thing, I thought somebody made the idea up to sell greeting cards and heart-shaped chocolates on Valentine's Day. But then it happened to me. I took one look at you, Kate Winton-Jones, and I fell in love."

His voice choked up at that moment, and she felt her eyes tearing up and imagined that every other person in that room was struggling with emotion too. Nick cleared his throat once more and said, "Kate, I don't know what the future holds. I hope it brings us nothing but joy and happiness. But this I do promise you. I loved you the first moment I saw you, and I will love you until the end of my life. I promise you to be the best husband I know how to be, the best friend I know how to be, and God willing, the best father I know how to be. On this special day, in front of our friends and family, I want to say it loud and clear. I love you." Then he raised his glass and said, "To love."

It was an unusual toast. In her experience of weddings the toasts were to things like the bride, the bridesmaids and the happy couple. Who toasted love? And yet, at this moment, the toast seemed so perfectly right, as all of them raised their glasses and echoed, "To love."

She heard the echo of those words from the man holding her hand. As the afternoon wore on there was laughter and back-slapping and more champagne and cake. She thought of all the weddings she'd been to that cost hundreds of times more than this one, and how much more fun she was having at Kate and Nick's very casual party.

She found a few moments to chat with Kate alone and was able to say, with all sincerity, "This is one of the best weddings I've ever been to."

"Thanks," Kate laughed. "This is absolutely the best wedding I've ever been to."

"This is probably a really inappropriate time to ask you this, but I need to ask your advice."

Kate immediately grew serious—Ashley remembered that in her professional life she'd worked for a foundation that coun-seled troubled girls. "Do you want to go somewhere private and talk?"

She shook her head, smiling. "No, it's nothing like that. I feel so stupid even asking you this, but I found this article online." She paused. "No, wait, I have to go back. When Aunt Millicent and Uncle Duncan found out I was engaged to Eric, they were super excited. I don't know if you know this, but I've always been the person in the family that everyone thought would never amount to much. So, to find them actually thinking I had done this great thing was pretty awesome. Anyway, next thing I knew, Millicent was giving me," she glanced around making sure no one was in earshot and dropped her voice even further, "your Evangeline wedding dress. The one you didn't wear."

Kate's eyes opened wide. "Wow. I never even thought about what happened to that dress. Well that's great, it's a beautiful dress."

"It is. It is a beautiful dress. But, please don't think I'm crazy, but I read this article online that said that dress is cursed."

If she'd expected Kate to laugh and assure her that the curse was a piece of nonsense to get more eyeballs on a gossipy website, she was wrong. Kate was quite serious when she said, "I don't know where they picked up the story, but it's true."

"It's true that my wedding dress is cursed?"

Kate paused for a moment, then replied, "It was a truly awful moment. I was being fitted for the dress and a seamstress accidentally pricked me with a pin. Evangeline started yelling at this poor seamstress – not because I was hurt but because a tiny spot of blood seeped into the silk. And don't worry, they were able to get it out. But suddenly the seamstress rose up like something out of mythology or a horror film and cursed both Evangeline and the dress and then stormed out. Most of it was in some other language, but she told us in perfectly understandable English what she had done."

Ashley could feel her eyes growing round. "So, do you think that's why you didn't get married? Because the dress was cursed?"

Kate shook her head. "First, I don't believe in curses. But then, I don't believe in ghosts either, but that doesn't mean I wouldn't be terrified if I saw one. You know what I mean?"

Ashley nodded. She knew exactly what she meant because that was her whole approach as well to this cursed dress thing.

"I did end up running away before my wedding, causing a lot of upheaval and ill will. But I'd do the same thing again in a heartbeat. The truth is, it wasn't the dress that was cursed. If anything was cursed, it was my engagement to Ted. Ted is a great guy, but he is so much happier with Marlene. We were both fooling ourselves." She took Ashley's hands in her own and gave a quick shake. "If you love Eric, and Eric loves you, then no pissed off seamstress is going to get in the way."

If you love Eric, and Eric loves you... "Right. Of course you're right. I'm just having, you know, jitters."

"Perfectly normal." Then she put her head to one side. "But then, I didn't have a single jitter leading up to this wedding. My whole body and my mind and my heart all said yes every time I thought about this day. I know I'm doing the right thing, and marrying the love of my life." She glanced across the room at Nick. "In my opinion, a curse doesn't stand a chance against true love."

THE FERRY back to the mainland was about to leave and all the wedding party including the bride and groom were lined up along the dock ready to board. Ben suddenly turned to Ashley. "You know, I've never even seen the island. There's another ferry back in two hours. You want to stay?"

Ever since she'd held hands with him during the wedding, she'd had this sense of unreality as though this were a magical island and the regular rules didn't apply. She had a strange feeling that he felt the same way, and that once they boarded the boat back to the mainland, the magic would disappear. Still, she hesitated.

She watched Nick and Kate board the boat, laughing and holding hands and she nodded. "Yes. I want to walk on these pretty little streets and go to the botanical garden. I wish I was wearing my hiking boots; it seems like there's great hiking here."

He took her hand and once more she let him. "Come on, then, let's go exploring."

It was a steep, upward climb to the botanic garden and a couple of times she stopped to admire the view, mostly to catch her breath. But there was something so magical about the island. The tiny houses all looked like storybook cottages, the air was warm and the sea sparkled all around them. Above the gardens was the Wrigley memorial. They wound their way along the paths, admiring the plants and flowers, and then climbed up to the memorial which offered a stunning view of the island and the ocean.

They didn't talk much, and their usual joking camaraderie was strangely absent. She felt that he was preoccupied, and in truth she was a little preoccupied herself.

As they stood side by side, staring out at the view, she said, "I'm so glad we came today. That was one of the nicest weddings I've ever been to." She turned to him. "Thank you for bringing me."

For an endless moment he looked at her, and she couldn't look away. She thought of those words Nick had said about the impact of looking into the eyes of someone you're falling in love with. He moved closer until they were almost touching. "Ben, I…" She had no idea how to finish the sentence and then it didn't matter. He slipped a forefinger under her chin, raising her face. She didn't resist. This moment had been inevitable since that awkward almost kiss at her engagement party. She knew that whatever happened, she couldn't go through the rest of her life without at least having kissed Ben.

He put his mouth on hers and for a moment she felt nothing but the warm pressure of his lips against hers, and the feel of his body adjusting to fit against her. Her arms came up and wrapped around him, and then, like a delayed reaction, fireworks exploded all over her skin. She'd never felt so alive, or so wanting, and suddenly the light, easy kiss transformed into this mind-blowing meeting of bodies and minds and souls and she was helpless to stop it. She felt swept away on a tide of passion she couldn't even understand, never mind control. He pulled her closer. She pulled him closer. She wanted to climb inside his skin. As her mouth opened to him and he slid his tongue inside her, she wished that he was inside everywhere. They kissed for a long, long time and when he pulled away slowly she found that she was breathless.

He looked down at her with a sad, rueful expression. "I was afraid of that."

She knew exactly what he meant. There was no point in talking about what had happened. Nick had talked about bombs going off in his chest and she knew exactly what he meant.

She clutched at her engagement ring, pushing her thumb against it until the sharpness hurt, to remind herself of her reality, the diamond-hard reality that she was engaged to another man.

CHAPTER 15

*A*shley and Ben were a lot quieter on the ride home than they had been on the way down. There was so much she wanted to say to him, to ask him. So much she felt coming from him. All this unspoken emotion was stifling her so, without even asking him if he minded, she pushed the top down on the car. It was dark and the rushing wind on the freeway was cold, but she didn't care. She wanted to blow away all the craziness of this day. Maybe if she could replace the feel of his warm arms around her with cold, biting air, her skin would forget how he'd felt.

And maybe if she brushed her teeth enough times, she'd scrub out any memory of his kiss. Yeah, that was going to happen.

When they drew closer to the Carnarvon estate, she put the top back up. The silence seemed huge. Like a cavernous, empty space waiting to be filled. She said, "It's not only me, is it?"

"No."

"I still remember that horrible crazed obsession I had for you when I was a kid."

He reached for her hand. "It was the most flattering thing

that ever happened to me."

"Thanks. But I'm not a kid anymore."

"I know."

"When I was fifteen it was one-sided."

"Mostly."

"Now—?"

"Now, it's not."

At least she had that to hang on to. "But me being engaged isn't the only thing between us, is it?"

His hand tightened briefly on hers. "No."

She didn't feel like asking endless questions and receiving one-word answers so she remained silent. It was a while before he spoke, but when he did she heard pain in his tone. "I had to promise my agent I would stay away from women for a year."

"A *year?*"

"Yes." He blew out a breath. "You know about Vanessa. That story is slowing down, but she's a great media manipulator. I could maybe date a woman quietly if she had no public profile.

"But my engagement is all over the place."

He nodded. "Grace Van Hoffendam is almost as good at handling the media as Vanessa is."

"And if I left Eric for you, that wouldn't look good for your career." She sounded bitter, she knew she did, but she didn't care. She felt bitter.

Ben had shown up within days of her engagement. She wondered now whether, if Eric had waited a week to propose, she'd have been so quick to say yes.

As though he'd read her mind, he said, "The timing really sucks for both of us."

"I know."

"There are lots of good, practical reasons for you to marry Eric."

"And only one reason not to."

"Can we not do this right now? Please? I want to finish my

screenplay, and have coffee with you every morning by the pool, and continue our driving lessons."

A rush of emotion threatened to choke her, so she merely nodded.

WHAT WAS HIS PROBLEM? Ben wondered as they drove the last few miles toward home. Fear, that's what. He was scared. When he had been twenty and Ashley was only fifteen, pushing her away had been the right thing to do. But now? Now that she was a woman of twenty-five and he masqueraded as a man of thirty? Did he really believe that his career was more important than his happiness? Because Ashley made him happy. More importantly, she made him authentic.

This was not something that happened a lot in LA; he'd noticed that the more successful he became, the more people told him how wonderful he was. They piled on effusive compliments, called him a genius, gifted, brilliant, groundbreaking. After a while, it was too easy to believe the flattery. But not with Ashley. From the moment she had scoffed at his clichéd female character and his stilted dialogue, he had begun imagining her as the person sitting in the darkened movie theater watching his story unfold.

When he crafted a line he felt was funny, he wondered whether she would laugh. If the scene was sad enough, could he make her cry? Maybe she wasn't a mermaid or Cinderella. Maybe she was his muse.

He was lost in thought when they pulled up in front of the gate. He found the remote and punched in the code. The gates silently opened, letting them in, and then just as silently closed behind them. She drove forward, her capable hands controlling the vehicle. She pulled into his parking spot behind the pool house and turned off the engine. It was so quiet.

She glanced over at him, her eyes seemed big and luminous and glistening with emotion. With hurt. She passed him the keys. "Thank you for coming with me to the wedding," she said softly.

He did not know what he'd been thinking, but he couldn't let her go, not like this. "Ashley—"

She threw open the car door, not letting him finish. "I have to go."

He reached out and grasped her wrist. "Ashley, please, I'm a fool. Everything I said back there was about me being scared." And now he felt foolish even admitting such a thing.

She shook her head and pulled her wrist out of his grasp. "No. You're right. The wedding and all that emotion made me a little bit crazy. Thanks for bringing me back to earth. Really."

By the time he was out of the car, she was already striding away.

He cursed silently as he watched her walk away. He was convinced he had never done anything in his life that he would regret more. But what could he do? It was late, she lived with her mother. It wasn't like he could barge into their cottage and have a confrontation. He would have to wait until the morning and hope that she came for her regular swim. Maybe by then he'd think of something brilliant to say to her, something that would convince her that he did want her in his life.

His night was extremely unproductive. He couldn't sleep, he couldn't work, he couldn't get his mind to settle. He'd been around long enough now to see two sides of Ashley. He saw the woman who was so accustomed to hand-me-downs and left-overs that she had unconsciously begun to think of herself as second best. He also saw the outwardly tough, I-don't-give-a-shit persona that she wrapped around her like armor.

But there was a version of Ashley that he thought perhaps only he could see. The woman who saw through pretense because she had grown up with so much of it. The woman whose basic honesty and decency made him want to make the world a better place for her. He wanted her to be number one for a change. But was he ready? Was he really ready to take a woman who was engaged to a guy who might be an entitled twit, but who, on paper, looked like one hell of a catch? Was he going to try and lure her away from her engagement? And offer her what. Was he even ready to settle down?

Maybe he dwelt too much in the world of fantasy and fairy-tale and screenplays that had definitive endings, but for Ashley he wanted a big fanfare of a happy ending. She deserved that. More than she deserved to wear her mother-in-law's cast-off engagement ring, or her cousin's fiancée's discarded wedding dress. When Ashley got married, he wanted her to have everything exactly, perfectly, for her.

He got up early. He hadn't slept well anyway. He calculated time zones and realized he could reach his parents while they no doubt sipped Prosecco on a terrace somewhere in Tuscany. He tried his mother's cell phone and sure enough she answered right away. "Ben," she cried when she heard his voice. "We were just talking about you."

"Were you saying nice things?"

"Of course we were. But we don't have very many nice things to say about that stupid actress who is making your life hell over there. How is that going?"

Trust his mom and dad to keep up with Hollywood gossip from half a world away. "It's fine. The story's dying down. These things always do."

"Well, don't do anything to fire it up again."

He winced, knowing that was why he'd called her. "Lester says I have to stay away from women for at least a year." He hadn't meant to say that. And he knew his mother well enough to imagine she would poke away at each word, dragging out his meaning.

"And are you?" Yep, she'd nailed it.

"No."

She made a soothing mother noise. "Do you want to talk about it?"

Of course he wanted to talk about it. And with someone whose advice he could trust. "Mom? Do you remember Ashley Carnarvon?"

"Of course I do. She's Millicent and Duncan's niece. And I see she's getting married to one of the Van Hoffendams. Those old, wealthy families do like to intermarry." There was a silence. Even across thousands of miles he could hear the gears whirring in her head. "I remember that girl had a real crush on you back when you were a teenager." She didn't put a question mark at the end of teenager, but it was implied.

"Well, she's not a teenager anymore."

"And the crush?"

He felt his eyes squint half shut as though the light coming in through the pool house window was too intense. "I think the crush is mutual this time."

There was music playing somewhere on his mother's side of the world, some Italian pop song. He waited for his mother to speak and she took her time answering. "What about her engagement?"

"Eric van Hoffendam is a dick."

"And yet, apparently, Ashley has agreed to marry this dick."

"I know. She's making a big mistake."

"And if she were free?"

"What do you mean, if she were free?"

"I remember her as a surly teenager who wanted to be accepted in that family so badly it made my heart ache. Now she's found acceptance in a prestigious, wealthy family. She will most likely end up with a lovely home, be a member of exclusive private clubs, she'll be asked to sit on charity boards... everything in her life will suddenly be first-class. Are you asking her to give all that up? And if she does, what are you offering?"

"Whose mother are you? Aren't you supposed to want the best for me?"

"Of course I want the best for you. I also want to make absolutely sure that she isn't desirable to you for the wrong reasons. First, because she lives in the same place as you and you see her all the time, and second, because she has the added attraction of being forbidden fruit."

"I know. I thought of that. I don't think that's it. She's the most honest person I've ever known." He grinned in memory. "Brave, too." Briefly, he told his mom about the gun incident. After she finished scolding him for letting one of his actors wave a real weapon around in front of a window, only then could she appreciate Ashley's role.

Then he told her about how Ashley had read some of the dialogue for his female protagonist and slammed it without pity.

"You let her read your script?"

"Some of it, yeah."

"You never let anyone read your work until it's finished."

"I know, but she's got incredible insights. And, like I said, because she's so honest I know she's not blowing smoke. If she's so quick to tell me when something isn't working, then I know that if she actually compliments me on a scene, or even a line of dialogue, that she's sincere. Do you have any idea how hard that is to find in this city?"

"I can imagine. So, to recap: your agent, one of the top in the business, told you to stay away from women for a year for publicity reasons. Instead of following his advice, you have fallen for a woman whose engagement has been written up in the *New York Times*."

"It's kind of a mess, isn't it?"

"Does she intend to end her engagement and run off with you?"

"I don't know. I haven't asked her to."

"Why not?"

"Because I'm scared."

"Scared you'll lose her? Or scared you'll end up trapped?"

"If I knew the answer to that, maybe I could get a full night's sleep."

"Darling, I cannot tell you what to do. But you already broke that girl's heart once. Be very careful before you do it again."

"What about my heart?"

She chuckled softly. "I think maybe you need to listen to what it's trying to tell you."

He wondered if it wasn't only his heart that was trying to tell him something. "You know what's weird? They got engaged like a week before I got here and the wedding's only a few weeks away. You go to those society things all the time. Don't they usually take a year or even two to plan?"

"Absolutely. Is there some reason for this hurry?"

He rolled his gaze. "She's not pregnant, if that's what you mean."

"That's not the only reason for a fast marriage."

"What are the other reasons you can think of?" He'd racked his brain but hadn't come up with much. But he wasn't as well versed in social niceties as his mother was.

"I don't know, could one of the parents be ill perhaps? And they want to see their son settled?"

"Everybody looked pretty healthy to me." He thought back to the engagement party. "There was something strange going on at the engagement party, though. I walked into the conservatory and accidentally overheard a conversation between Duncan Carnarvon and Charles Van Hoffendam." He relayed as much of it as he could remember. "I didn't really understand what the judge had to do with it, but I went looking for him afterwards and he wasn't at the party."

"That's odd. He and Duncan Carnarvon are very close. I

would absolutely have expected him to be at Ashley's engagement party, unless he was out of the country or something."

"I asked Millicent and she seemed upset that he wasn't there."

"You think the judge has something to do with the quick marriage?" She sounded very puzzled. Which was exactly how he felt.

"I wish I could figure it out."

"Darling, I know you make a great deal of money because of your active imagination, but don't let it run away with you. This is real life, not one of your movies."

"I know. And if I had any brains, I would pack up my computer, throw my socks and underwear back in my bag, and head back to my house." The paparazzi had stopped hanging around his place. He knew the coast was clear for him to return. It was Ashley who was keeping him at the pool house.

"That would probably be the sensible course of action."

"Thanks, Mom. Love to dad."

"Are you going to be sensible?"

From the corner of his eye he saw a flash of green and a splash as Ashley dove cleanly into the pool. Was he going to be sensible? "Hell, no."

While Ashley powered back and forth up and down the length of the pool, he brewed another pot of coffee. And he decided to pay an old family friend a visit. Maybe his mother was correct and he was making up stories, creating a mystery where none existed. But he'd been thinking for a few days that he wanted to talk to the judge. He had a key scene in his script involving a judge and he wanted to get the details right.

He phoned Judge Bailey's house and the judge himself answered. When he identified himself, Ben heard pleasure in the older man's voice as he said, "It's good to hear from you, Ben. How are your parents?"

"They're having a fantastic time in Italy. I just got off the phone with them, as a matter of fact, and they asked me to give you their best."

"Isn't that nice. Next time you're talking to them, tell them I asked after them both."

"I will. I was thinking of taking a drive down your way today."

"It is a beautiful day for a drive. Would you like to come for lunch? Martha usually fixes something special on Sundays."

"Can I bring a friend?"

The old man chuckled. "A lady friend?"

"Duncan Carnarvon's niece, Ashley. I've been staying at the pool house on their property. I'm teaching her how to drive."

"Ashley Carnarvon. Well, well." The tone was gruff, possibly sarcastic. But, after a moment, the judge said, "Of course. I'll tell Martha we'll have two extras at lunch today."

"Look forward to seeing you, sir."

He picked up the two mugs of coffee, and, as was his usual morning custom, slipped on dark glasses and carried the drinks out beside the pool. Either he'd misjudged, or she was doing a longer workout today, so he settled in one of the loungers, sipping his coffee and enjoying the morning until she was done.

"I could get used to this," she said, wrapping a big towel around her and walking over to grab the cup of coffee he'd prepared for her. Her feet left wet prints on the cement edge by the pool. She acted exactly as she always did with him. That steamy kiss and their painful conversation in the car last night might never have taken place. She settled beside him and lay back, letting the sun warm her wet skin. "It is such a beautiful day. And I have the entire weekend off."

He knew this, because she'd told him yesterday. Her boss had misunderstood when she'd ask for Saturday off to go to a wedding on Catalina Island, and given her the whole weekend off.

He was glad to see that there was no weirdness between

them after the kiss yesterday and their strained conversation in the car. One of the best things about Ashley was that she didn't hang on to old grudges. He had the strangest impression that when she jumped into the pool each morning it was a kind of rebirth, as though she washed off the old feelings and started each day brand new. He looked over at her. This was one of the highlights of his day, he realized, these few minutes they spent together over coffee before they both got on with their days. He said, "Do you feel like a drive to Manhattan Beach? I want to visit Judge Bailey. You could drive."

"Why are you visiting the judge?"

"He's an old family friend and I want to pick his brains about a plot point in my script."

"I don't know. I've got a lot to do for the wedding."

He was surprised how much he wanted her to come with him. "Come on. It's a gorgeous drive down the coast, and he invited us for lunch."

"You told him I was coming?"

"I said I might bring a lady friend."

Her lips twitched. "You actually said lady friend?"

He shrugged. "He's an old-fashioned guy."

She sent him a glance from under spiky wet eyelashes. "He's not the only one."

"So? Will you?"

"Be your driver? Or your lady friend."

He leaned closer. "Be both."

She settled back in her lounger, moving her back around until she was more comfortable. "I don't know. I could drive down the coast and enjoy a nice lunch, or I could go with Millicent and my mother to choose floral arrangements for the wedding."

He made himself equally comfortable and pulled his shades down his nose so he could look at her over the top of them. "No contest."

CHAPTER 16

*A*shley wasn't completely sure why she chose a driving lesson and lunch with a man she barely knew over picking the flowers for her own wedding, but when Ben had asked her to go with him, she knew which she'd rather do.

She understood that she was acting crazy. She was engaged to Eric. So why could she not stop thinking about that kiss? It wasn't just a kiss. She'd shared lots of kisses with other guys. None of them had ever made her feel as though something monumental had shifted. As though her life would never be the same. From one damn kiss?

He'd been as affected as she had, she knew he had. So why did he refuse to even talk about it? All that *I have to finish my script and not date women for a year* crap made her blood boil. Did he think kisses like that happened every day?

She had an awful moment when she wondered if every kiss was like that for him. If the magic wasn't because of the two of them, but if he brought the magic himself. It traveled with him and he doled the magic out to lucky women now and then.

She showered and changed into a demure sundress, suitable for Sunday lunch with an older couple, and she knew that she was a sucker for punishment. But the truth was, life was about to change. Soon, Ben would go back to his life as a Hollywood screenwriter and she would begin her new life, married to Eric. It still seemed completely unreal to her. Eric acted as though nothing would change, but there was already a realtor sending them listings of suitable houses and she'd been invited to attend a meeting of The California Charitable Women's Institute, whatever the hell that was. With Millicent.

Between them, Millicent and Melody and Tasmine-the-professional-bridesmaid/wedding coordinator seemed to have everything well under control. The truth was, when she went along to choose anything from the catering menu to the songs to be sung at the wedding service, she felt like the least important member of the party. If asked her opinion, she usually deferred to whatever they felt was best, mostly because she really didn't care.

She was used to doing whatever other people wanted. So, if her mother and future mother-in-law chose the flowers for the tables without her, she imagined everybody would be perfectly happy.

And she would enjoy one more day with Ben. She knew there weren't very many left before everything changed.

He'd been her dream man at fifteen. At twenty-five, he was still her dream man. Maybe that was her tragedy. She was letting her dream man go, and marrying her playmate.

She knew, however, that if Ben asked her, she'd go with him. Ashley had scoffed at love, at the idea of soul mates and true love for years. The truth, however, was that she had fallen in love with Ben when she was fifteen years old. Now, she loved him in a newer, more mature way. She hated to admit the truth, but she'd met the love of her life when she was a teenager. He hadn't wanted her then, and it looked like he didn't want her now.

She was a realist. She would enjoy his company for the little time remaining to them, she'd help him as much as she could with his screenplay, enjoy every minute she could have with him, and then, when he left, she'd get on with her life as best she could.

She had no illusions that she was the love of Eric's life, so she didn't feel like she was misleading him. He seemed to think that they could have a good marriage, and she was determined to do her best to be a good and faithful wife. Maybe that was enough. Maybe fairytales belonged in old musty books that got packed away in attics when little girls grew up.

Of course, no hint of her feelings showed on her face when she walked up the path and met Ben for what would probably be their last driving lesson.

Ben had also dressed up in order to lunch with Judge Bailey and his wife. He was freshly shaved, he'd taken a little time with his hair, and he wore a good pair of jeans and a shirt with sharp creases.

His eyes warmed when he saw her. "You look beautiful," he said.

But not beautiful enough to change his life for, she thought. "Thanks."

He tossed her the keys and she took her accustomed spot in the driver's seat, then they headed out once more. She never grew tired of driving the coast road, of the endless surf and curving bays. Being a sunny Sunday there was a fair bit of traffic, but she didn't care. Ben and she could talk about anything and everything. He made her laugh, he made her think, he made her feel as though what she said mattered. As though he listened. As they drew into the Manhattan Beach neighborhood where the judge lived, she said, "One of Eric's best friends from college lives down here. The parents go away a lot so Eric and his buddies come down here to party."

"Pretty nice playground."

She followed his directions and pulled into the long curving drive of a Spanish-style mansion with red tile roofs and white stucco walls. Palm trees dotted the perfect green lawns and behind the house she could see the sparkling ocean.

The woman who answered the door didn't seem like a maid. She was a middle-aged Latina woman with a big, welcoming smile. She didn't wear a uniform so maybe she was the house-keeper. Ben seemed to know her. "Maria, how are you?"

"I am very well Ben. It's good to see you. The judge and Mrs. Bailey are very happy to have company today." She extended her smile to Ashley. "Please, come in."

She led them through the quiet house, decorated in a more modern fashion than Ashley would have imagined, and out to a covered patio with a stunning view. The judge and his wife sat side-by-side reading pieces of the Sunday *Times*, and Ben strode forward not waiting to be announced. "Judge Bailey, it's so good to see you."

The older man rose. He must have been close to eighty, but he stood tall and straight, with dark, piercing blue eyes under a shock of white hair. He had the permanently tanned look of a golfer or a sailor. He and Ben shook hands and patted each other on the shoulders simultaneously. Then Ben turned to the older woman. "Martha, it's so good to see you." He leaned down and kissed her cheek.

He turned with practiced politeness, "And I think you both know Ashley Carnarvon? Duncan and Millicent's niece."

The judge offered her a slightly cool look as he held out his hand. "Of course. I haven't seen you for some time." She had no idea how to respond to that, so she simply smiled and shook his hand.

She'd met his wife even fewer times than she'd met the judge, so she bypassed the cheek kissing and shook the older woman's hand.

The four of them sat outside and the judge and Ben did most of the talking. The judge offered them wine, champagne, a sherry, or something stronger. She asked for iced tea, explaining that she was driving. Ben sent her an approving look, and also opted for iced tea. She understood the source of the approving look when Martha said, "Ernest tries to use guests as an excuse to drink wine at lunch time. Even though his doctor has told him it's bad for him."

"Only trying to be a good host," the judge replied.

They all sipped iced tea and then a young maid brought out a wheeled tray containing salads, which she put in front of each of them. This was followed by crab cakes, and then roast chicken and vegetables. Dessert was fresh fruit and coffee. Over coffee, Ben got the judge talking about case law, in particular the case law surrounding the history of crooked cops in LA. "Do you mind if I tape this?" he asked, pulling out a small digital recorder.

"No. Of course not." The judge settled back and talked. He was like an encyclopedia. Reeling off facts and names and dates. Ben let him talk, interspersing the odd question.

At the end of probably half an hour, Ben said, "This is fantastic information. Thank you so much." He switched the recorder off. "Now, I'll stop dominating the conversation with work. Martha, how are things going at the gallery?" Before Martha could answer, he turned to Ashley. "Martha is an expert in the post-Impressionists."

Martha shook her head at him. "Not an expert, dear. Merely an enthusiastic amateur."

Once more, Ben turned to her. "Martha's being modest. She studied art in Paris and when she returned to California, she brought with her a passionate love for Picasso and the cubists. She developed one of the best private collections in the United States, and has donated a number of works to museums around the world."

Martha smiled modestly. "I don't believe that one should

hoard art for one's own pleasure. It's meant to be enjoyed by everyone."

All of a sudden the judge lifted his fist and banged it down on the table so the coffee cups jumped and clattered. It was like a clap of thunder in the middle of a peaceful, sunny day. Everyone turned to stare at him.

His face was ruddy with emotion as he glared at Ben and then at her. "I don't know what your game is here, but I don't like it." Ashley glanced at Ben to find him looking as bewildered as she felt. She wondered about dementia, but the way the judge had rattled off all those figures from old cases made her wonder.

There was awful silence for many seconds and then Ben said, "I'm not sure what you're referring to judge, but I'm not aware of any game."

To her horror, the judge pointed one of his bony fingers right at her chest. "And what about you, young lady? You know anything about a game?"

She shook her head, wishing she could turn tail and run. "I came with Ben. That's all."

The judge grew even redder in the face. He still glared at her unwaveringly and she felt that if he were still sitting behind the bench she'd be sentenced to life imprisonment, or worse. "And what about your fiancé? Where is Eric Van Hoffendam?" He spat the words.

She swallowed nervously. "His house, I guess." She glanced over at Martha, wondering if they should leave so the judge could have his afternoon nap or whatever he clearly needed. But she found Martha also staring at her, a sad expression in her faded brown eyes.

"What's Eric got to do with this?" Ben asked.

"You really don't know?" the judge replied, but again he was looking at her.

A horrible sick feeling blossomed in her belly. She felt like she was getting in trouble and she didn't know what she'd done wrong. She shook her head mutely. The urge to run grew stronger by the second. If she hadn't returned the car keys to their rightful owner before entering this house, she thought she might actually have scampered out of there, never to return.

"Ernest, please," Martha said softly. "Remember your blood pressure."

The judge turned to his wife. "If this young lady truly doesn't know, then I think she has a right to learn what kind of a man she is marrying, before it's too late."

She spoke up. "I don't understand, I didn't even realize you knew Eric."

"I've known his father, and before that his grandfather, for years. Good, decent men. But that youngster, that hooligan is another story." He poked his finger at her again. "He ought to be in jail. And if it weren't for you, he would probably be on his way. I may be old, but I'm still a power to be reckoned with."

Eric was many things, but he wasn't a criminal. She couldn't imagine what he could have done. And then she thought of his history of pranks, some of which could be pretty elaborate, and she wondered if he'd hired strippers to sing at the judge's last birthday or something. She glanced around, but couldn't see any topiary gardens that had been disfigured. "Did he pull one of his pranks on you?"

The redness in the judge's cheeks grew deeper and she could see purple veins like a map of the world's rivers. He threw down his napkin and rose on unsteady feet. "You can decide that for yourself." He strode into the house, shouting, "Maria?"

The housekeeper arrived, walking calmly from another part of the house. "Yes, judge?"

"Get somebody to set up that surveillance video from the vandalism incident," he snapped.

A worried frown creased her forehead. "Are you sure you want to see that right now, Judge?"

"No, I don't want to see it, but I'm going to show it to this young lady."

By this time, Martha had followed them into the house. She and Maria exchanged a glance and then Maria nodded. "I'll set it up for you in the media room."

"Thank you."

"Do you know what's going on?" Ashley asked Ben.

"I am completely mystified." And yet, she didn't think he seemed as shocked as she was. She kept her gaze steadily on his face and he shifted and glanced away.

Martha said, "Well, I suppose we should get this over with."

She led them down a flight of stairs and along a short corridor to a home theater. A movie screen dominated one wall, and black padded chairs looked like comfortable seats from which to watch a movie.

Maria was already fiddling with machinery when they got there. They sat in a row. Martha, then the judge, then Ashley, and beside her, Ben. She wished she hadn't eaten so much at lunch. Her stomach felt tight with nerves. The judge hit a remote to dim the lights. Before he pushed play, he said, "Martha and I were away for our wedding anniversary and so we gave the staff the weekend off. Neighbors, a few doors down, were also away. They have a son who has been known to throw parties in their absence.

"They've never been able to control him, so they seem to ignore his behavior, I suppose, in the mistaken belief that what they ignore doesn't exist. As I said, our staff had had the weekend off. But we have an excellent security company and because of the number of valuable paintings and artifacts in this house, there are security cameras everywhere." He sighed heavily and glanced at her from under bushy eyebrows. "If this is truly something you are unaware of, I am very sorry."

And then he pressed play. She could see a swimming pool and surrounding it a few carved marble statues. She didn't know mythology well enough to identify them, but she was certain that they were most likely rare and valuable. The garden was lit and spotlights highlighted the statues. A date and time stamp appeared in the top right-hand corner of the picture. A week before he'd proposed.

After maybe ten or fifteen seconds of watching an empty pool and the silent garden, there was movement on the right-hand side of the screen. Four guys staggered into the frame. Tall, blonde, and drunkest of them all was Eric. There was no sound, so it was like watching a silent movie. She could see the four of them: Eric, Toad, a guy he called Slade, and the college buddy whose parents lived nearby. His name was Dave. The four of them were laughing, Eric was drinking what looked like rum straight out of the bottle. He passed the bottle to Toad.

She couldn't stop watching Eric. She felt her fingernails dig into her palm, wishing he would go away, that they'd all go away. There was more joking, and she saw Eric sidle up to a female statue that looked Greek, and serene, and had wings. It was a goddess or an angel, she couldn't be sure, but to her horror Eric walked over and grabbed the statues naked breasts like he was feeling up a real girl.

Then he started to dry hump the statue. The other three were doubled over with hilarity. Please, she said to herself, please just go away. Let this be all there is to it. But of course, Eric loved to show off, and if he had an audience he was inclined to escalate his pranks.

Dave, the one who lived near here was waving his arms, pointing at the house. Next thing she knew, Eric was unzipping his pants and while the four of them watched from their comfortable movie recliners Eric peed in the swimming pool.

"I am so sorry," she said, as though Eric were somehow her responsibility.

But the horror was only beginning. Dave joined his college buddy and also relieved himself in the pool. Then the four drunken delinquents staggered around trying the doors to the house. She imagined they were looking for more booze. She could see them twisting the doorknobs.

They began banging on the doors and she could see that they were yelling to be let in. Finally, the neighbor boy picked up a stone and banged it against the glass panes of the French door. She suspected he had only meant to get the attention of someone in the house, but in his drunken state, he didn't know his own strength, and while they watched this awful silent movie, she saw the pane of glass break. For a second the four men froze, and then Dave put his hand through the broken pane of glass and opened the door.

"Don't you have an alarm?" she cried.

"It's a silent alarm. The second that glass broke the security company was alerted and they were on their way."

The picture jerked and now they were looking at the wall inside the house. Three paintings hung in a row. Ashley didn't know much about art, but these looked like something you'd see in the Met or the Louvre or somewhere famous. They all had a Picasso-like look to them and her heart began to pound with dread. Peeing in the pool and dry-humping garden statues was one thing, but breaking and entering jumped Eric and his buddies up to a whole new level. What were they thinking? What were any of them thinking?

This was like a nightmare that wouldn't end. She knew something awful was about to happen and she wished she could wake up so she didn't have to know what it was going to be.

As she had dreaded, the four drunks ambled into the picture. At least Eric had already drained his bladder, so there was no possibility he could pee on the paintings. And he didn't.

He walked and squinted at all of them. Then he struck a pose, like a teacher, or a tour guide, and he began an animated discussion as he pointed to each of the three pictures. She had no idea what he was saying, but his three were once more laughing. He moved out of the frame and then, to her horror, he returned holding a Sharpie in his hand. "Oh no," she moaned. She wanted to cover her eyes but she couldn't.

He waved the Sharpie, and then, as she watched, helpless to stop the destruction, he yanked the top off the indelible marker and with great swoops of the pen, as confident as Picasso himself, he painted two boobs on the chest of the middle painting and added round circles for nipples. At this point, something happened. She suspected the security people arrived, for, like actors in a silent comedy, the four of them froze, looked at each other in panic, then all began to run.

The judge turned off the picture and hit another button to turn up the lights.

Complete silence filled the room. It was Martha who broke it. "I brought that painting in Paris in 1963. It's not a Picasso, but a fellow artist and a very good friend of his." She sighed, as though she were at a funeral. "It's not always the monetary value, sometimes the value is in what a painting means to a person."

"Can it be repaired?" she asked in a small voice.

"I've had the painting sent to the top team of art restorers in California." She shook her head. "They're doing everything they can."

The judge spoke up, "Those paintings are like my wife's children. And I will not stand by and let anyone hurt my wife."

His hands formed into fists. "That boy should be in jail. I was fully prepared to press charges. Then Charles Van Hoffendam asked for a meeting."

He glared at all of them.

"I've known Van Hoffendam for years. But that wouldn't have stopped me. That punk of his needs a sharp lesson and he'd get one in jail. But Grace and Charles came to see us. They offered to pay damages, pay to have the pool drained and cleaned, to pay for the restoration, but it's not the money that matters. That boy should be punished. However, they convinced us he was trying to change."

"They really both looked ill when they saw the video. They dragged Eric over to see us the next week and he apologized to us," Martha added. She was clearly a softer-hearted woman than her husband.

The judge continued. "He's promised to clean up his act. He's getting a job, I understand, and then they informed me he was marrying a nice girl from a good family, a Carnarvon. Well, Martha and I allowed ourselves to be persuaded. When we saw the engagement announcement in all the papers, we assumed you knew about your future husband's antics."

She licked her lips. They were dry as though all the moisture had been sucked out of them in the last few minutes. All she could think was that date stamp. The convenient timing of Eric's proposal. "What if I don't marry him? Will you send him to jail?"

The older man looked at her steadily for a long moment, then shook his head. "I am going to give you some advice, young lady, and I'm an old man who has seen far too much. What I do, or the Van Hoffendams do, or anyone does should have no bearing on your conduct. But you should think very carefully." He waved a hand at the now black screen. "Is this the man you want to marry?"

They left soon after that. As they were leaving, Martha said, "I'm so sorry," as though it was somehow her fault that Ashley should end up having such an awful day.

CHAPTER 17

*S*he and Ben got into the car and he didn't even offer to let her drive. She was shaking too badly.

He started the engine and headed back the way they'd come, so happily, a few hours earlier.

For a long time, neither of them said anything, then she cried, "You knew, didn't you?"

He glanced over at her. "No. I didn't."

"Then why, today of all days, would you want to have lunch with the Baileys of all people? Are you trying to ruin my life?"

"No. Of course not."

"Do not lie to me. Enough people have lied to me in the last few weeks." Everything was coming clear to her now, as clear as the vision of Eric defacing a nice old couple's priceless art collection. No wonder Eric had suddenly wanted to marry her, and that his parents had welcomed the union with open arms when they'd never acknowledged her existence previously. "The date stamp on the video footage was a week before Eric proposed to me.

"How could I have been so stupid? I knew everything was rushed and it wasn't natural for Grace and Charles Van

Hoffendam to treat me so nicely. Except that they needed me. I was his Get Out of Jail Free card. You knew something. What was it?" She almost screamed the last words. She and Ben had become close over the past weeks. They'd pretended they were friends, but she'd fallen in love with him. She'd believed, even if he didn't share her feelings, that he'd be honest with her. Now it felt as though he were part of a grand cover-up.

He jerked the wheel and pulled over to a viewing area. He got out of the car and she did too, slamming the door behind her.

Near the beach, a huge rock heaving with sea lions was the big viewing area attraction, but she didn't have much interest in the antics of sea creatures right now. There were a couple of land creatures who had her full attention.

Ben stared out to sea for a moment and then turned to her. The wind whipped at his hair and he pushed it back impatiently. "At your engagement party, I accidentally overheard a conversation between Charles Van Hoffendam and Duncan Carnarvon. It didn't make a lot of sense at the time, but they mentioned the judge. I thought it was strange that he wasn't at your engagement party, and something about the tone of that secret meeting's been bothering me ever since."

"Uncle Duncan knows about this?"

Ben looked at her almost with pity. "I don't know how much he knows, but he obviously knows something. Frankly, it was a bit of a pissing match with both of them claiming the other one's kid was getting the best deal."

"A deal? I'm a deal? Like trading stocks?"

"To those two, everything's business. You know that."

"Why didn't you tell me any of this?"

"What was there to tell?"

She was angry, so angry. With him, with Eric, with the judge for ruining her happy day. With everyone named Carnarvon or

Van Hoffendam. "I feel like you set me up, taking me down there today."

"Honestly, I didn't mean to."

"But you knew something was up." She felt the tension knot her shoulders. It was giving her a headache. "I am not a character in one of your screenplays, where you get to play God and manipulate people into horrible situations to see how they'll react. This is real life. My life. You had no right to interfere."

Suddenly, he grabbed her shoulders. "If Eric Van Hoffendam is a bad person, then you should know that before you marry him. I don't want you to make a mistake."

She wanted to hit him she was so mad. She pushed right up into his face, "Oh, yeah? And what are you going to do to stop me?"

He glared at her, his eyes fierce with longing and then he pulled her to him, hard. He kissed her, not with finesse and fireworks like he had the day before, but with pure passion, anger and frustration all mixed up. She felt herself respond to the dark emotions and then, realizing what she was doing, yanked herself out of his arms.

"Stop this," she yelled. "Just stop."

Then she got back into the car. A moment later, he slid into the driver's seat and they pulled back into traffic. They didn't speak at all on the drive back home.

When they pulled into his spot, it was like a replay of the night before. He said, "Ashley, wait."

She said, "Go to hell."

WHEN SHE STORMED into the cottage, she entered a scene that was cozy, domestic and cheerful. She slammed to a halt as she saw her mother, looking happier than Ashley had seen her in a long time. With her was a guy about her mother's age who actually didn't look like a complete loser. A stunning bouquet of flowers sat on top of the coffee table and Eric and Tasmine sat side by side in front of it, both bent over Tasmine's table computer.

She was so stunned she simply stood and stared.

"Ashley," her mom said, coming forward, all girlish and happy. "I want you to meet Chuck. He's going to be my date for your wedding, if that's okay."

Chuck seemed like a nice man. He got to his feet and shook her hand. "Congratulations on your marriage. Your mother and I have been, um, spending some time together. I thought you and I should get to know each other."

"Great. Sure." She shook his hand. Everyone was looking at her but she wasn't sure what more they wanted. "Are your intentions honorable, Chuck?"

They all cracked up like she was Tina Fey. "Indeed, they are. I'm a dentist. I'm divorced, no children. I, um, think your mom's a wonderful person."

Okay, she needed to get her head out of her ass and be happy for her mother. At least someone's life was on the upswing. She dragged up a smile. "I think so, too."

Melody pointed to the bouquet. "That's a sample of the flowers we chose for the tables. Aren't they gorgeous?"

"Stunning."

Then she turned to Tasmine and Eric. "And you two are...?"

"I have to get gifts for the groomsmen. Tasmine's helping me choose."

"Perhaps a replica of a garden statue would be nice," she said through gritted teeth. "Or maybe something from the art world. What do you think, Eric?"

He glanced up, looking busted, but Tasmine either didn't notice the tension or pretended not to. "We were sort of thinking cufflinks. Traditional, but with a modern twist."

Ashley simply stood there, her gaze fixed on Eric until he

dropped his head and stared at the ground. "Maybe we could finish this later," he said to Tasmine.

"Sure, absolutely." She rose and gave Ashley a quick hug. She whispered, "The last couple weeks before the wedding are always the toughest," and then she was gone.

"Why don't we take a walk to the beach," Eric said once Tasmine had left.

The pair of them walked to the beach. He didn't tease her or try to take her hand, he didn't even ask where she'd been. He shuffled along, his head down, and when they got there, he turned to her. She didn't say anything, simply stared at him.

He seemed to be trying to read her expression, probably trying to figure out how much she knew. He said, "What was that about? Back there?"

"What do you think it was about?"

He let out a breath. "You know, don't you? You were never supposed to know."

"I know that you defaced a priceless work of art if that's what you mean. And then got engaged to 'a respectable girl from a good family,' to keep your ass out of jail."

He looked so scared that for a moment she thought he might cry. "I can't believe I did it. I mean, I seriously can't believe that was me. I was so drunk—"

"I should throw this engagement ring back in your face," she snapped.

He seemed to deflate. His blue eyes weren't twinkling with devilry, they seemed older and a little sad. "Yeah," he admitted. "You should."

"You know what will happen if I do that?"

He nodded. Swallowed. "I'll go to jail."

She turned and started back toward the cottage. "Are you breaking up with me?" he yelled after her.

"I'm thinking about it," she yelled back.

That was bad enough. Worse was Grace Van Hoffendam's

tearful visit. "Ashley," she said, "You've been with Eric for ten years. You know he's a decent person. He gets carried away, but that's why being married to you will be so good for him. Please don't send him to jail. I'm begging you."

She walked the beach and she tried to imagine Eric in jail. She couldn't.

She might have talked it over with her mother, but Melody was happily dating Chuck and already talking about turning Ashley's bedroom into her TV room.

She didn't swim Monday morning. She didn't want to see Ben through the window. She didn't want to have coffee with the man who'd teased her with a glimpse of happiness and then snatched it away again.

By Tuesday, she was damned if she was going to give up swimming because of him. She donned her green bikini and stomped up to the pool, determined to tell Ben that she wouldn't be having coffee with him anymore and she no longer needed driving lessons. But she didn't need to say any of those things.

When she got to the pool house, Ben's car was gone. She peered in through the window, but there was no sign of him or his laptop. Could he be working at a coffee shop? She hadn't wanted to see him or talk to him, except that now he wasn't here, she really wanted to do both. She had some things she needed to say.

She dug out the hidden key from under the third pot and, after knocking, let herself in. It didn't take her two minutes to discover there was no one there.

Ben had left, without even saying goodbye.

CHAPTER 18

$\mathcal{I}$n the distance, Ashley could hear the twinkling melodies of the orchestra her aunt and uncle had hired to play music suitable for well-heeled guests as they settled themselves and waited for the wedding ceremony to begin. Her mother had gone ahead to the big house, and she really needed to be getting there too, as uncle Duncan would be waiting to walk her down the aisle.

She'd sent her bridesmaids on ahead. She needed a minute. One minute, completely for herself. She glanced around the bedroom that had been hers for most of her life, and that she wouldn't be returning to after today. In her younger years, she'd decorated her full-length mirror with various stickers.

In the top corner was stuck a strip of photos from a photo booth. She and Eric were probably seventeen. She pulled the strip down and studied the black-and-white images. It was vintage Eric, doing a rapper pose in one, making ridiculous faces in another, and finally smiling into the camera with his most charming and serious expression on his face, while his hand grabbed her chest. He was still a joker, still that seventeen-year-old boy more comfortable pulling a prank than acting like a man.

Tucked in the other corner of her mirror, hidden beneath a Hang Loose sticker, was another picture. It was the only picture she'd been able to get that summer that Ben came to stay for a few weeks. He was tanned, grinning away, with his arm slung around her fifteen year old self.

She stepped back and gazed at herself in her wedding dress, the dress that had been designed for another bride, cursed before it was ever worn, and now hung on her like a bad perm.

She crossed the room and pushed up the sash window, lifting her face to the sunshine and breathing in the smell of the ocean. Back in her teen years, she's used this window to get in and out of her room, either to go to parties she wasn't supposed to go to or to sneak over to Eric's place. She sat on the windowsill, lifted her legs and swung around. The dress followed her, bunching around so she felt like a fish trapped in a huge net.

Above the sounds of Mendelssohn she heard the purr of a car engine. It was a nice sound, the sound of someone going places. She listened, and the sound grew louder. She turned her head.

The Ferrari was recently washed, she noticed, and it gleamed in the sun. He had the top down, exactly the way she liked it. He wore dark glasses like a spy or superhero. The car drew closer and stopped right outside her window. Ben said, "You planning to jump?"

There was about a foot between where her satin shoes ended and the neatly edged lawn began, but still she shook her head. "What are you doing here?" It was hard to sound casual when her heart was banging so hard she thought she might pass out.

"I came to talk to you about your driving."

She raised her eyebrows. "Are you offering me a lesson? Now?"

He removed his sunglasses so she could see his eyes, blue, full of fire and amusement and a big dash of tenderness. "No. I don't think you need any more lessons. I think you're ready to take the wheel of your own life, don't you?"

Before she could answer, her name was being called. "Ashley? Are you here?" It was the world's most perfect bridesmaid, Tasmine, hired to make sure everything ran smoothly, including getting the bride to the altar on time.

"Keep the engine running," she said to Ben. Then she turned, dragging the dress back inside, and called, "Tasmine? I'm in here."

When the chirpy bridesmaid entered, saying, "It's time," she turned her back.

"Help me get out of this dress."

For a second Tasmine stared at her in shock. Then she walked to the window and glanced out. When she turned back, they stared at each other for seconds that felt like hours and then she nodded, sharply, and as efficiently as she'd helped Ashley into the dress, she now helped her out of it.

Ashley grabbed a pair of jeans and the first T-shirt she could put her hand on, scrambled into a pair of socks and running shoes, grabbed her purse and gave Tasmine a hug.

"What do you want me to do with the dress?" Tasmine asked, her arms full of billowing white fabric.

Ashley was already halfway out the window when she turned back, laughing. "Why don't you wear it? Isn't it time to stop being a bridesmaid and become a bride?"

Then she dragged off Grace's cast-off engagement ring and tossed it. Tasmine grabbed the ring. "Good luck."

Their gazes connected. "You too."

Ben had moved over into the passenger seat while she'd been changing, leaving the driver's side empty and the door open. She jumped in and slammed the door shut. Before she hit the gas she said, "Are you sure about this?"

"When fate offers a happy ending, only a fool doesn't take it."

"Am I your happy ending?"

He leaned forward and pulled her to him. "You are my beginning and my middle and my happy ending. You are the love of my life," he said, and then he kissed her. When he pulled back, he said, "And now, I suggest you floor it."

And so she did.

Thanks for reading *Secondhand Bride!* Continue following this magical dress in *Bridesmaid for Hire*, Book 3 in *The Almost Wives Club* series.

A Note from Nancy

Dear Reader,

Thank you for reading *The Almost Wives Club* series. I am so grateful for all the enthusiasm this series has received.

I hope you'll consider leaving a review and please tell your friends who like contemporary romance or romantic comedies.

Review on Amazon, Goodreads or BookBub.

Join my newsletter for a free prequel to my *Vampire Knitting Club* series, *Tangles and Treasons*, the exciting tale of how the gorgeous Rafe Crosyer was turned into a vampire.

I hope to see you in my private Facebook Group. It's a lot of fun. www.facebook.com/groups/NancyWarrenKnitwits

Until next time,
Happy Reading,

Nancy

ALSO BY NANCY WARREN

The best way to keep up with new releases, sales, plus enjoy bonus content and prizes is to join Nancy's newsletter at NancyWarrenAuthor.com or join her private Facebook group www.facebook.com/groups/NancyWarrenKnitwits

The Almost Wives Club

An enchanted wedding dress is a matchmaker in this series of romantic comedies where five runaway brides find out who the best men really are!

The Almost Wives Club: Kate - Book 1

Second Hand Bride - Book 2

Bridesmaid for Hire - Book 3

The Wedding Flight - Book 4

If the Dress Fits - Book 5

The Almost Wives Club Box Set - Books 1-5

Take a Chance series

Meet the Chance family, a cobbled together family of eleven kids who are all grown up and finding their ways in life and love.

Chance Encounter - Prequel

Kiss a Girl in the Rain - Book 1

Iris in Bloom - Book 2

Blueprint for a Kiss - Book 3

Every Rose - Book 4

Love to Go - Book 5

The Sheriff's Sweet Surrender - Book 6

The Daisy Game - Book 7

Take a Chance Box Set - Prequel and Books 1-3

The Vampire Knitting Club

Paranormal Cozy Mysteries. When Lucy inherits her grandmother's knitting shop in Oxford, she discovers secrets and solves murders with the help of some special undead amateur sleuths.

Tangles and Treasons - a free prequel for Nancy's newsletter subscribers

The Vampire Knitting Club - Book 1

Stitches and Witches - Book 2

Crochet and Cauldrons - Book 3

Stockings and Spells - Book 4

Purls and Potions - Book 5

Fair Isle and Fortunes - Book 6

Lace and Lies - Book 7

Bobbles and Broomsticks - Book 8

Popcorn and Poltergeists - Book 9

Garters and Gargoyles - Book 10

Diamonds and Daggers - Book 11

Herringbones and Hexes - Book 12

Ribbing and Runes - Book 13

Cat's Paws and Curses - A Holiday Whodunnit

Vampire Knitting Club Boxed Set: Books 1-3

Vampire Knitting Club Boxed Set: Books 4-6

The Vampire Book Club

A middle aged witch gets sent to Ireland to run an unusual book shop.

Crossing the Lines - Prequel

The Vampire Book Club - Book 1

Chapter and Curse - Book 2

A Spelling Mistake - Book 3

The Great Witches Baking Show

The Great Witches Baking Show - Book 1

Baker's Coven - Book 2

A Rolling Scone - Book 3

A Bundt Instrument - Book 4

Blood, Sweat and Tiers - Book 5

Crumbs and Misdemeanors - Book 6

A Cream of Passion - Book 7

Gingerdead House - A Holiday Whodunnit

The Great Witches Baking Show Boxed Set: Books 1-3

Toni Diamond Mysteries

Toni is a successful saleswoman for Lady Bianca Cosmetics in this series of humorous cozy mysteries.

Frosted Shadow - Book 1

Ultimate Concealer - Book 2

Midnight Shimmer - Book 3

A Diamond Choker For Christmas - A Holiday Whodunnit

For a complete list of books, check out Nancy's website at NancyWarrenAuthor.com

ABOUT THE AUTHOR

Nancy Warren is the USA Today Bestselling author of more than 90 novels. She's originally from Vancouver, Canada, though she tends to wander and has lived in England, Italy and California at various times. While living in Oxford she dreamed up The Vampire Knitting Club. Favorite moments include being the answer to a crossword puzzle clue in Canada's National Post newspaper, being featured on the front page of the New York Times when her book Speed Dating launched Harlequin's NASCAR series, and being nominated three times for Romance Writers of America's RITA award. She has an MA in Creative Writing from Bath Spa University. She's an avid hiker, loves chocolate and most of all, loves to hear from readers! The best way to stay in touch is to sign up for Nancy's newsletter at NancyWarrenAuthor.com or www.facebook.com/groups/NancyWarrenKnitwits

To learn more about Nancy and her books
NancyWarrenAuthor.com